Pitcher

KRISTY MARIE

For Jaime and Kathrine.
You've seen the worst sides of me and yet,
you still remain my friends.
You deserve a medal.
Or at least a book dedicated to you.

Every story has a villain.

In our story, the villain is not a person but an emotion.

Our villain is fear.

Fear of the unknown.

Fear of losing the most important thing in our lives.

Each other.

But we have hope. Because for every villain lies a hero.

Wrong.

Our story doesn't have a hero either.

Our story sucks.

We suck.

We allowed fear to dictate our lives to the point we became stagnant—hopeless—as we watched each other move on and fight the feelings between us.

No one comes to our rescue in this story.

In this story, we are the villains and the saviors.

Enjoy the shitshow that is our relationship.

Pitcher

Chapter One

Anniston

I'm not sorry.

Not even a little bit.

The asshole deserved it.

"Anniston, do you have something to say to Preston?"

I smile sweetly at the round man, known as the principal of Hawkins Middle School, home of the suck-tastic tigers. I've been trapped in this mauve-colored room that smells like bad decisions and mold for over an hour now. I'm bored and I have yet to see the point of Principal Taffert's stern scolding. Can't he see Preston is a lying, fourteen-year-old, sack of dog shit?

Why is it only me who sees his true colors? Me, who sees the rotting of his evil soul as he sits all surly, holding a bag of ice to his face.

"I…" I chance a look at my grandpa, his hands clasped over his dirt-stained overalls. He's a good man. He doesn't deserve the granddaughter he was left in charge of. He deserves a good girl, one who acts like a lady. Unfortunately, he isn't so lucky.

With a devilish smirk, I meet the glare of Preston and his haughty mother next to him and smile as sweetly as I can. "I wish Coach Carey would have taken longer smoking his cigarette in the supply closet so I could have broken more than your nose, assface."

"Anniston," my grandfather says on a sigh.

"Hines," Principal Taffert says over Preston's mother's gasp of horror. "As much as I hate to do this, I must suspend Anniston for the rest of the school year. We can't encourage this kind of behavior." He looks at me and frowns. "Even from a girl."

That's right, Preston! A girl beat your ass. How's that taste? I bet it tastes bitter, much like big, salty tears of defeat. Little bitch.

"I understand, John. Grace and I will handle this at home."

I don't even spare my grandfather a look. All I'm looking at is the bump on Preston's nose that I hope will haunt him the rest of his life. Maybe he'll remember it the next time he decides to be a bully.

"I'm sure you will," Principal Taffert responds before clearing his throat and addressing me. "Anniston, I hope to see a changed young lady next year. Use this time to reflect on your actions and decide on the type of woman you want to be."

I want to be an ass-kicker, John. A Katniss freaking Everdeen.

"I will, sir."

I will hone my right hook and make sure I go for Preston's balls the next time he dares breathe in my direction.

Standing, my grandfather motions for me to follow.

"We're so sorry," he says to Preston's mother who is still sitting like she has on the tightest pair of underwear imaginable. She manages a "humph," and I almost want to take a swing at her for birthing such a horrible human, but I don't.

Hines McCallister is a patient, God-fearing man, but if you get on his bad side, he will act first and ask for forgiveness later.

Before I can get us into any more trouble, I slam the office door behind me and follow like the dutiful granddaughter I am.

"Did he tease you about your mother or father?" he asks when we leave the building to walk to his truck, which is parked in a visitor space in the front of the building.

I shrug at his back. My grandfather has worked hard to build a life for me. He's sacrificed so much to make sure I have everything I need. I want to protect him from the ugly truth, like he's always protected me.

"Anniston…," he prompts softly and oh so patiently.

I'd rather go back inside and deal with Taffert than to break my grandfather's heart.

"Last week," I swallow, "in computer lab…"

"Last week, what?" he urges.

I sigh. "I had a hard time typing, and he saw."

Gently. You must be gentle with Hines McCallister.

The lines in his forehead crease before he frowns, looking much older than a few minutes ago. "Was it a flare up?"

I nodded. "I couldn't control it, and I started to cry." I shrug like it wasn't nearly as bad as it was. "He started making jokes—"

"That little shit made fun of your condition? A child with cerebral palsy?"

Oh hell. I knew he would be mad.

"It's okay, Grandpa," I soothe, hurrying to clasp his hand in mine. "I took care of it. He won't make fun of me again."

He grumbles but lets me pull him to the truck. When he unlocks my door and helps me up like a gentleman, I smile.

"Thank you, fine sir."

That makes him laugh.

When he's in and has the barely working a/c on blast, I cut him a sneaky grin. "So what are we going to do since we have the rest of the day off?"

He snorts. "We—" He motions back and forth. "—are going to finish my deliveries since I was interrupted."

I cringe. "I'm sorry." I really am. "I wasn't thinking when I hit Preston. I just don't like feeling weak."

The man that has been the only father figure in my life grasps my chin between his strong fingers. "Don't be sorry for standing up for yourself. You hear me?"

I try to nod, but I don't get very far with his firm grip on my chin.

"You're not weak, Anniston McCallister. Not. At. All."

And this is why I try to behave. For him. For my grandma. These two people are the only ones who care about me.

"Okay," I whisper, straightening up and plastering a smug smile on my face. "Now, whose day do we need to make with this dairy fresh milk that I had to get up at 5:00 a.m. to acquire?"

Yeah, it was bad. Cows stink. So do goats and other animals that live on a farm. Old McDonald should have gone with fish. They are much less maintenance.

"The Von Bremens. They need an extra delivery this week since their boys are home from school."

Really? The elusive Von Bremen boys you say?

"Well, what are you waiting for, Pops? Let's get this delivery done. We have *Jeopardy* to watch."

"Are you sure you want to wait out in the truck?"

I look around the upscale home, notice the baseball bat leaning against the front door of the massive brick home, and decide to leave the elusive Von Bremen house a mystery.

"I'm sure," I tell him, but then add quickly, "I might get out and stretch my legs, though. If that's okay?"

"Okay," he says after a minute, eyeing the backyard as if something evil lurks behind it. "But stay close to the truck."

An easy smile and a promise that he'll return soon sends him up the driveway with woven baskets hanging from his arms. I unbuckle my seat belt when he's out of eyesight and ease out of the truck. The cobblestone driveway is uneven underneath my sandals, and the humid breeze plasters my clothes against my skin as soon as I shut the passenger door.

Madison, Georgia is known for its sweet, family-like atmosphere. At a mere two thousand people, no one is a stranger—except for the Von Bremens. All we know is they keep to themselves and run a large insurance agency in the city. Rumor has it that Oscar Von Bremen, the head of the insurance empire, has twin boys that he ships off to boarding school in the city every year.

I've lived in this town my entire life, and I've yet to actually see them. A girl I know said she saw them once at a gas station and they were, and I quote, "smoking hot." Smoking hot boys in this town are like rare unicorns; mostly because we grow up with the same faces since daycare.

Small towns can be a problem when you're trying to reinvent yourself, or when trying to escape the nickname "Mac." It's not a cute nickname born out of love, trust me. Kids at school call me Mac because they think I want to be a boy.

I can't help I'm better at sports than most of the boys. I also can't help the fact they can't throw up a block or dodge my fist... like Preston.

I am who I am.

And if I'm really being honest, I don't give two shits if the kids at my school like me.

I don't need friends.

I'm perfectly fine entertaining myself.

With nothing left to do but stare at the baseball bat against the door, I get back in the truck. Then I hear the garage door rise, and a voice I will never forget booms across the driveway.

"Thad, I would rather drown in ball sweat than go to Michelle-whoever's birthday party with you."

The air surrounding me seems to grow thick as I hold my breath, waiting to finally see what *he* looks like. My gaze darts everywhere until I find them. There, standing as identical replicas, are two boys around my age. Both are the same height as one another, but where one has short, dark hair, the other has a baseball hat covering most of his. Even with the hat, I see the dark curls furling out from underneath. The girl was right. They are smokin' hot, but it's the one with the basketball and the smart mouth who gives me goosies.

"We have to go," says the one without the hat. "It's her birthday, Theo."

So *his* name is Theo. It has a certain ring to it.

Theo scoffs and makes a disgusted face at his brother.

"Is this the girl that sounds like she's hocking a loogie every time she laughs?"

I nearly laugh out loud at his description of the girl and wonder who she is. I'm not friends with any Michelles, or girls that sound like they are hacking up phlegm when they laugh.

"She's our cousin, Theo. Mom expects us both to be there."

His cousin? My stomach clenches with barely contained laughter. Surely he knew that. Surely he's just getting on his brother's nerves by acting like he's clueless whose party they are supposed to attend.

"No thanks, bro. Tell Mom I have mono." He looks pensive for a moment. "Or chlamydia. She definitely won't want to explain that to her country club friends."

The brother looks to the sky as if he's praying before losing his temper. "Can't you do me *one* favor?" he snaps, snatching the basketball from his brother and shooting it from his spot beside him. It makes a swooshing sound before bouncing back to the guy with the hat. He scowls and gives his brother the middle finger.

"Letting you borrow my shirt is a favor," he says, all smug before shooting the ball and barely hitting the backboard. Glaring at the board like it offended him, he continues, "Attending this nightmare of a party is a fucking charity donation. Don't confuse the two, Brother."

You would think after the day I've had, I would be done with assholes, but that's not the case. Call me curious—and hungry, apparently. Since when does my stomach flutter when I get hungry?

"I don't even know why I'm arguing with you. Mom will make you go. You're fourteen, not twenty."

Fourteen? Interesting. He is my age.

"Why do you think Mom cares if we go? She'll be too busy with her sister gossiping about God knows what. She won't even realize we're not there." He shrugs like he has the world all figured out and gave it instructions to adhere to his standards.

"Maybe I want to go," Thad says, lowering his voice as if he's trying to convey something to his brother. "Maybe I want to go and see Heather…"

Theo laughs, not getting sucked in by Thad's obvious feelings for this girl. "By all means, go 'see' Heather. I'm sure she'll be ecstatic to have another loser follow her around while she burps out the ABCs with her horrible laugh."

Finally, his comments get to his brother. "Heather is not the one who hacks," Thad argues, but stops when he sees the shit-eating grin on his brother's face. "You're an asshole," he spits. "One day you're gonna think about someone other than yourself."

The boy makes a disbelieving scoff.

"And when you find her... I hope she breaks your heart." With that parting remark, Thad heads back through the garage and disappears.

Theo, unaffected by his brother's comment, takes another shot at the basket and misses. Again.

"You know," I holler, hopping out of the cab and strutting up the driveway like I didn't just watch the two boys fight, "the goal of basketball is to actually get it *in* the net."

If I thought I was going to get a big reaction out of him, I would have been wrong. Theo's head doesn't whip around to face me. He simply retrieves the ball and takes another shot, barely sparing me a glance.

"I was wondering," he starts off low and hypnotic, a slow grin pulling across his face, "if you were here to sell Girl Scout cookies or talk to me about Jesus." Theo raises his brows, and I don't know if I want to hit him or smile. "What's it gonna be, little Miss Goody-goody? You got cookies or a Bible? I'm hoping for some Thin Mints."

This ass. This cute, ridiculous ass.

"I'm not a Girl Scout," I say, snatching the ball out of his hand, gripping it with my fingers, and shooting effortlessly from my hip. It goes in—of course—and I flash him a smile that conveys all the smugness in the world.

"*That's* how you make a free throw, sweetheart."

Why I said that, I have no idea. Call it a challenge. Something about this boy sparks a fierce competition within me.

His grin is slow and dangerous. "Touché, little Brownie."

I shrug. "It's all in the hips." I toss him the ball and frown. "Maybe you can practice and suck a little less next time?" I say, already turning and heading back to Grandpa's truck. My job here is done. I taught the boy how to shoot. Somewhat.

"What's your name, Michael Jordan?"

I grin, not turning around. "Anniston," I call back, almost to the truck.

He's silent at first, but then… "Hey, Ans?"

I turn at the new nickname that makes me feel all kinds of girly.

"Want to come to a party tonight?"

The smile on my face dies along with his dreams of becoming a basketball star.

"Can't," I say, as I reach the truck.

"Why not?"

His voice is much closer, and I whip around to find him right behind me. His deep blue eyes are piercing when he grins—attempting to be charming—and a dimple forms in his right cheek. Yeah, that dimple is a killer.

I shrug at the rude and insanely cute boy in front of me.

"I'm probably grounded."

His smile ratchets up his face. "Sounds like my kind of girl."

Sounds like my kind of guy too, but I would never admit it to him.

"What'd ya do?"

Again, I go with a shrug before locking stares and admitting, "I broke a boy's nose."

It takes two seconds for him to react. Two seconds for him to throw his head back and belt out a laugh that bounces off the bricks, making the sound seem melodic.

"No shit?"

I nod slowly.

"Hang out with me tonight, Anniston. I'll even let you pretend to show me how to shoot hoops, not that I care if I'm any good. I play baseball."

He plays baseball… Of course he would have to play my favorite sport.

"What position?"

He doesn't hesitate. "Pitcher."

Why God? Why must he be a pitcher?

"Are you a southpaw?" I ask, referencing the baseball term for a left-handed pitcher. I figure he is since he shot the basketball from his left side.

One side of his lips pull up, but he doesn't answer me. "Hang out with me, Ans, and maybe I'll tell you. I promise you'll have fun."

Before I realize what I'm doing, I agree. "I'll talk to my grandfather."

"That's my girl."

I ignore the fluttering feeling when he calls me his girl. Instead, I smack the ball from his grip and dribble up the driveway before he can catch me.

This friendship is either going to be a huge disaster or one of the best mistakes I've ever made.

Turns out, it's both.

Chapter Two

Theo

Four years later…

Wary glances are cast my way as I push past the guests without an *excuse me*. These nosey motherfuckers should be grateful I checked my attitude at the door. My purpose here is not to kiss ass or show the good people of Madison what a respectable young man I can be today.

Hines and Grace were family.

I came here to pay my respects, and to get my girl. "Did you find her?" With no greeting, my brother gives me a worried look as we pass each other through connecting hallways.

I swipe a hand through my hair—not having a hat on feels strange. "No."

I force out a breath, my eyes scanning the mass of people for any sight of her.

"You don't think she..." Thad trails off, afraid to finish his question.

"She wouldn't do anything stupid." The confidence in my voice is fake. I don't know what is going through Anniston's head today. The only family she had is dead.

Her mother.

Her father.

And now both of her grandparents.

Two days before she walks the stage as salutatorian for our High School, Anniston McCallister will smile at two empty seats in the crowd.

She's all alone in this world.

My heart pounds in my chest as panic settles in.

"Keep looking," I bark at Thad, pushing past him. I don't give a fuck if we're at a wake or not. Ans needs us, and if I have to upend this entire funeral home to get to her, I will. Consequences be damned.

"Check the caskets if you have to," I add, totally serious, before blazing through the crowded hallway on the hunt for my girl.

I shouldn't have let her drive herself. Anniston was insistent she would be fine and there was no sense in me going out of my way to come get her. She promised to wait for me in the parking lot, but when Thad and I arrived, she was nowhere to be found. The funeral home director said he spoke with her soon after she arrived before excusing herself.

She hasn't been seen since.

Two women ease out of the bathroom with frowns, catching my attention. "Is she in there?" I ask the younger one who looks back at the closing door. I don't need to clarify who she is; they know. Anniston McCallister is the only granddaughter of Hines and Grace McCallister. In a small town, everyone knows about her tragic entrance into this world. And now everyone knows how a tragic car accident left her the sole heir of their plantation.

"Yeah," the gray-haired woman breathes out. "She's not speaking to anyone."

I don't give her time to finish or thank her. I shove past them into the ladies' bathroom. Ms. Tate, a teacher from the public school that my father finally allowed me to attend, is standing at the stall door trying to coax Ans from the stall. "Sweetheart," she coos, "can you open the door?" When she spots me, she slides to the side, making room.

I rattle the handle. "McCallister, open the door."

I hear a muffled cry like she's been holding it in and hearing my voice popped the seal.

"Please, sweetheart, open the door." Ms. Tate's voice is soothing, but it's not what my girl responds to.

With a hand to her shoulder and a reassuring smile, I thank her for trying. She looks confused at my dismissal but takes the hint and leaves. When we're alone, I open the stall beside the one Ans has barricaded herself in and step up on the toilet to peer over the stall. On the bathroom floor, curled up in the corner and hugging her knees, sits my girl—the only person in this world that I can't live without. The ache in my chest feels like I've been hit by a pitch, a stinging sensation only an ice bath will soothe.

"Open the door, Ans, or I'll climb over."

She never looks up, but her head jerks in a firm no, making the soft curls bounce along her black dress.

I let out a heavy sigh.

"Have it your way," I warn, already hoisting my body weight on the divider. Both legs sweep over the side of the wall gracefully, and I linger on the edge a moment before I drop in front of Anniston.

"Good thing you're small enough to wedge in beside the toilet—yuck, by the way—but at least I didn't land on you."

My backhanded skinny compliment goes unnoticed, just like my plan to talk to her as usual flushes down the proverbial toilet. Anniston's soft cries are swallowed up by her dress, and my stomach clenches with the fear my girl won't be the same after this.

"They're gone," she mumbles, never looking up. "All these people keep telling me to call if I need anything." She hiccups, finally lifting her head up to meet my gaze. Blue eyes, swollen and streaked with harsh red lines, blink back at me. "But what I need, nobody can help me with." I squat down and reach for her when she continues. "I have no one anymore."

I snag her arm and pull her along the floor and wrap her in a bruising hug. "That's not true," I promise with something clogging my throat.

She cries into my shirt.

"You have me, Ans. You'll always have me."

I swear it. She'll never be alone. Her cries become harsher, and I hear the door to the bathroom open and close quietly.

"Do you hear me, Anniston?" I push her back and grab her quivering chin and force her to look at me. "You have me. You will *always* have me. Nothing will ever separate us. Do you understand?" Her lip trembles, but she nods. "Now, you're going to get up, dry your face, and we're going to leave."

She tries to argue, but I shush her with my finger. "This is not about appearances. We can come back later for you to say your goodbyes. You're not a parade float. You don't owe these people a smile or a sweet story. You got me?" She nods, already looking stronger. "We're going to your house and packing your shit."

Her eyes go wide. "What are you saying?"

I tuck a strand of hair behind her ear. "I'm saying we're going to find an apartment between our colleges. You're going to live with me."

"But—"

I cut off any excuses about me staying on campus to room with the baseball team by pulling her to her feet. Fuck the baseball team and the school. If they want me to win them a championship, they'll be flexible.

"I won't leave you," I promise with a stroke of my fingertip. Her lips turn down, and she fights back another round of tears.

"Don't make promises you can't keep." She sniffles, the glimmer of hope outweighing the sadness.

What she doesn't know is that, even if her grandparents were still alive, I would make the same promise. This girl is mine. I will never let her go.

Not now.

Not ever.

"Who says I can't keep my promise?" I taunt, trying to lighten the mood.

She shrugs, vulnerable and insecure. "We're friends, Theo. You don't have to feel guilty. You're destined for a life bigger than Madison. I won't be the one to stand in the way of your dreams."

If she wasn't so delicate at the moment, I would shake her. Full-on shake the shit out of her. Is she crazy? Does she not see the hold she has on me? Yeah, we're friends, but something more has been brewing under the surface all these years. Something neither one of us is brave enough to acknowledge.

"Don't argue with me, McCallister. You're moving in with me. Now, come on. The only time I stay this long in the women's bathroom is for head."

I lift a brow, teasing, and she pushes at my shoulder.

"You're disgusting." Her grin says she doesn't mean her words, though.

Pulling her close, I wrap her tight in my arms until she's strong enough to leave.

Two days later, donned in black and gold gowns, Anniston's name is called to walk across the stage. I see her rise, holding her head up high like she can take on the world alone.

But she doesn't need to because she has me.

And grudgingly, Thad.

I jump from my seat, ignoring the scolding look from the assistant principal, and leap off the stage, rushing into the crowd of parents. I find Hines's and Grace's seats before my brother reaches me, panting from rushing off stage too.

We fist bump, standing in the chairs, blocking the view of the parents behind us. We don't give a fuck though.

"Anniston McCallister. Congratulations, my dear," the principal praises.

Thad lets out a whistle that deafens me, and I whoop and holler, catching my girl's attention. Nothing will ever compare to the smile she flashes when she sees us standing in her family's seat. The pride stretched across her face is unparalleled when she shakes the principal's hand and holds her diploma up to me and Thad.

For the first time in a week, her eyes shine bright with happiness, and I know there is nothing I wouldn't do to keep it there.

Back to our seats on the stage, and a billion years later, graduation finally ends. Thad and I took our diplomas, waved to our parents, and then played on our phones through everyone's speeches. Yes, even Anniston's.

I'd heard it every day for the past two months. I could have given it for her. She wasn't mad. At one point, she even smiled at me before we threw our caps in the air. I could have blown off all of it, but it was important to Anniston. She worked hard through school, whereas I worked hard at baseball.

I understand the feeling of victory.

Today is Anniston's bittersweet victory.

She's done what she set out to do. Except, the people she did it for aren't here to witness her success. As her frown wavered from one handshake to another, all I could think about is how much we all need to get shitfaced tonight.

"Who wants to get blackout drunk?" I ask, pulling Anniston through the crowd toward my car.

"Me," announces Thad.

"Ans?" I prompt. She nods but then says, "Let's play a game too."

Motherfucker.

Thad and I both groan.

Anniston loves her games. Not that I don't enjoy a healthy dose of competition, but Anniston's games typically leave me rock hard.

"Nothing stupid," I compromise.

She crosses her heart with her free hand. "I promise, nothing stupid."

After the ceremony, we blew off invites to multiple graduation parties. Anniston had her heart set on a game, and well, I would have blown the principal if it would have made her happy.

"Truth or Dare?"

Hence the reason Thad and I are playing this bullshit—and *very stupid*—game on her living room floor.

"Don't you want to play something else?" Thad whines, taking a swig of the beer that Fred from the dilapidated gas station down the road slipped us.

"Come on! It's our last night as high schoolers. Live a little," she encourages.

We are living a little. Our livers are turning to mud as we speak. Anniston's grandfather left the liquor cabinet stocked… waste not, want not and all that.

Thad grumbles but ultimately goes with "Truth."

Bad move, Brother.

Anniston nearly squeaks with excitement.

"Is it true that Ashley Pollock had an asthma attack in the middle of giving you a blow job?"

I almost spit out my beer.

"I remember that shit!" I add to Thad's torment.

My stomach cramps remembering my brother coming home pale and quiet. I thought the fucker had been roofied.

"It wasn't an asthma attack," he argues, taking a healthy gulp of his beer. "She had an allergic reaction to my bodywash."

Anniston doubles over, heaving and snorting like a tiny pig. I'm grinning seeing her smile. I chance a look at Thad who's looking at her with the same relieved expression I am.

What the fuck?

My smile wanes as I watch him pull her close and tickle her, claiming she is being mean for bringing up that horrific memory.

Jealousy mixes with the alcohol in my stomach, and I refrain from snatching her from his arms. Everything about Thad holding Anniston pisses me off. Maybe it's because we are identical twins. Staring at him holding my best friend of years is like looking in the mirror. I can see the image, but I can't reach out and touch it. It's a reflection of everything I've craved from her since I hit puberty.

I found her first.

She's mine. Not Thad's.

So I do what I do best.

I act like an asshole.

"You showed her though." I hold my fist out for a bump he doesn't return. He knows what's about to come out of my mouth. "Her friend sure lapped up that cheap bodywash without a problem the following weekend."

Anniston sobers and pulls back to look at Thad.

"No, you didn't?"

Yes, he fucking did.

Thad drops his head and sighs. "It was a rough year. I was going through a few things."

Yeah, like being in love with my girl. It's no secret between us. I knew the minute Thad saw her, he wanted her. He tried playing the sweet brother, but what he didn't know is Anniston enjoyed the company of sin, aka me.

Before his embarrassing blow job story, he pined after Anniston, always texting her, always asking her to do shit with him.

I had to step in.

So Thad and I made a deal—neither of us could have her. We would be her friends. Her protectors.

Until now.

Until I found her on the floor in the bathroom.

"Poor Ashley." Anniston sighs. "I'm sure she was embarrassed too."

She wasn't. Two weeks later, after finding out about Thad and her friend, we discovered Ashley wasn't allergic to *my* bodywash. Bitterness is always a good fuck.

"It was a terrible thing to do," Thad explains. "I was a dick."

And horny.

And in love with a girl he couldn't have.

Love sucks like that.

Anniston grows silent and chugs the rest of her beer. "I think I'll go to bed. We need to get on the road early tomorrow."

To our new apartment.

Her gaze finds mine underneath a wayward lock of hair. "Stay with me?"

And that's why I'm a cheating son of a bitch. After her grandparents died, I knew our brotherly agreement was done.

Anniston is mine. Even if I don't deserve her.

I nod. "Go on. Thad and I will clean up."

She places a soft kiss to Thad's cheek before she gets to her feet and heads toward her bedroom.

I know the moment her door closes, Thad and I are about to have words.

He doesn't disappoint.

"You asshole."

I flash him an annoyed look. We all know I'm an asshole. This is not a new concept.

"Why can't I live with y'all?" he continues, undeterred.

Because he'll be in my way and I need to focus on my baseball career and Anniston.

"Your school is too far from the apartment we found," I lie.

Thad glares, snatching up our plates and leftover pizza from the floor. "It's not any farther than Anniston will have to drive."

Too bad.

"We only have two bedrooms."

We had no need for three.

"We could find a three-bedroom," he argues.

We could. We could also dress in pink tutus and sword fight, but we won't.

"It's too late. I already signed the lease." I shrug.

Thad's face turns red, the pizza box clenched in his hands.

"We had a deal, Theo."

I unfold from my position on the floor. "Circumstances changed. Don't be selfish. Anniston needs one of us with her. My school was closer."

Total bullshit and he knows it.

"I know what you're doing," he growls.

And I don't care.

Wrenching the pizza box from his hands, I sneer. "Don't get in my way, Brother."

Thad and I have never had a great relationship. We've always fought for individuality and attention. Whereas I branded myself quickly, he's struggled to figure out where exactly he fits in. Don't get me wrong, I love the bastard, but I'm tired of fucking sharing all aspects of my life with him.

I blame it on our mother.

Twins are for the elite. We were ideal for her to play dress up and parade around her friends. It was only when we weren't a replica of each other did we feel insecure. Someone had to capture the spotlight. Someone had to win. We couldn't always be equal. We couldn't always share our toys.

We couldn't be identical forever.

And we most certainly couldn't share my girl.

I flash my brother a look of regret. "She's always been mine."

"I think that's everything."

Cautiously, I raise my head from the trunk where I haven't been able to look away from the red pair of panties with tiny baseballs along the edges. Thad isn't here to see us off, and I understand. Last night I basically admitted that I don't care who I have to go through to have Anniston at my side, even if that person is my brother.

I stuff the pair of panties back in her bag. Anniston packed everything from her prom dresses to the crumbs under her bed.

She packed three times what I did. It's excessive and warrants a downsize. All I did was unzip one of her bags, intending on leaving some unnecessary shit here, but I saw the panties and all thoughts of downsizing scattered... along with my brain cells. Sure, I've seen some of Anniston's panties, but what I haven't seen is baseball ones.

These are lacy and girly. Visions of them sitting low on her hips have me sporting major wood right now. I can't fucking help it. My name literally belongs on the ass of those glorious underwear.

"Theo, yoo-hoo. Earth to Theo..."

Anniston's prompting forces my focus back to her face. Right. I need to answer her. Clearing my throat, I plaster on a smirk and pop back, "Are you sure you didn't forget the lint from the dryer? I think we have a few centimeters left in the car if you want to give the house one more sweep."

Eyes the color of my favorite blue Skittles narrow at my remark before they roll. "Did you pack your ADHD meds?"

Of course I did.

Wait.

"Ugh. Fuck," I groan.

I hate when she's smug.

"Don't worry," she chides. "We can stop back by your house on the way out of town."

She pats my shoulder almost arrogantly, and a rush of adrenaline hits me. I snatch her back, making her squeal in my arms.

"You're stuck with me for the next four years, McCallister. No take backs."

Slow, almost purposely, as if she needs a minute before she faces me, Anniston turns in my arms. Her eyes shine brightly in the sun before a quivering smile tugs at the corner of her mouth.

"No take backs," she agrees and swallows hard.

No take backs.

She just signed a deal with the Devil.

Anniston McCallister is mine.

All. Mine.

Chapter Three

Anniston

One month until our college graduation,
or Doomsday as we like to call it.

"Violet reports," I raise my voice so it sounds squeaky and pitches across to the kitchen, "that the highlight of the year is upon us!"

Theo, who is chest deep in the refrigerator, pulls back to glare at me. After more than three and a half years of living together, I've yet to miss an opportunity to embarrass him. And after the night I had, this morning's Daily Grind—the University's Paper—was exactly what I needed to brighten my day. He knows what's coming, and that makes this even better.

"She says, and I quote, 'Theo Von Bremen returns to the mound after the longest pitching rotation ever.'" I roll my eyes but continue.

"'His stellar—'" I mouth the word stellar and wiggle my brows. "'—pitching skills are unparalleled to anything Cantor University has ever seen before.'"

I glance at Theo who finally found what he was looking for—a freaking water—and smirk. "Violet needs to refresh her reporting skills. Cantor University has seen these *unparalleled pitching skills* before."

He flips me off while chugging his water, but I don't stop. "In fact, they've seen it several times. In the last ten years, Cantor University has had six players drafted to the MLB. The most in its history."

Violet has clearly been drinking the Von Bremen Kool-Aid. But whatever, so have most females on campus.

"Is Violet the girl who gave good head?" he asks me, his brows furrowed like he really has to think hard about it.

Must I always be the voice of truth in this relationship?

"Don't most of them give good head?" I find a piece of gum wedged in the sofa and throw it at him. It lands at his feet where he stares at it before cocking a brow in my direction. "It was a bad throw," I supply with an eye roll. I'm not the star pitcher here.

"I guess… head is head, but her name sounds familiar. Usually I don't remember names unless they were spectacular in some way or another." He shrugs unapologetically.

Unfortunately, I love this asshole.

Yep, I said it. I may be mocking poor Violet, but it's only because I'm jealous. And I really shouldn't be jealous if she gave Theo the best head he's ever had. Theo's personality is an acquired taste, much like wine. The package is beautiful on the outside, but the inside is sour until it rolls around the palate for a little while. Take it from me. I've loved Theo Von Bremen for years. Not months. *Years.* I loved him before he started going to the gym and bulking up. Not after puberty.

Before. Before his voice changed. Before we moved in together. Before we became best friends. Before he banged all the Violets of campus.

And it's all been for naught.

Granted, I've never broached the subject of more, but neither has he, so I left it. Guys are supposed to make the first move, right?

"I got it!" he shouts, finally picking up the piece of gum and popping it in his mouth.

Ugh. Why does he have to look so damn good working that strong jaw as it breaks down that rock-hard piece of gum into something thin enough to blow a bubble with? And why must that bubble draw my eyes to his lips, pursing as if he needs kissing?

Focus, Ans.

Completely focused—okay, fine, I'm semi-focused—I loosen the grip on my tablet and narrow my eyes, bracing myself for the epic blowie story that was worthy of Theo remembering Violet's name.

You will not get jealous. I highly doubt she was that epic.

"Violet was the journalism major that dated Reese all last year."

Oops. Sorry, Violet. My bad for thinking the worst of you. Keep up the hard work by reporting inaccurate statistics.

"Yeah, you remember we met her at his birthday party, and she said you were a saint for living with me." His smile morphs into a frown like he just realized she was insulting him.

Hello, Violet. My name is Anniston, and I think we just became best friends.

Not really. No girl is ever my friend. Unfortunately, I've always had a bff, and he has a dick. A big one. And because of said dick size and rumors of said dick size, I'm considered a threat. Or a frenemy. Same thing.

I've had my share of fake friends just so they could get closer to Von Bremen. I don't even try anymore. Theo and Thad are the only friends I need. Unless Violet wants to call me. I would totally buy her a coffee.

"Violet seems like a really nice girl," I taunt. "If she heard about what I went through last night, I think she would offer to buy me lunch today."

Theo groans, and it ratchets up my smile.

"I mean if she—"

"Do not bring it up," he cuts in. "Last night was your fault." He glares at me and takes another swig before punctuating each word individually. "All. Your. Fault."

You would think women are more easily embarrassed, but that's not true here. In this house, the man turns red faster than I do.

"I told you not to order the fish tacos."

"No. You said you *wouldn't* order the fish tacos."

I try to hide my grin.

"You did *not* say it gave you explosive diarrhea!"

At his outburst, my stomach clenches and I fold over laughing for the millionth time.

"It didn't give *me* diarrhea," I clarify.

"Oh no," he corrects himself. "You said it gave Thad diarrhea the last time y'all were there." He eyes me with a look of betrayal. How would I know it would happen again? Thad could have had a stomach bug a couple of months ago. It's completely possible.

"Who eats fish tacos anyway?" I scrunch up my nose. "You should have ordered the beef ones like we always do. Then I wouldn't have had to open the windows and ask Ms. Carmine down the hall if I could use her shower."

Okay, so I feel a little bad about it. But really, it could have been a virus this time too.

"I wanted something different! Brody said they were good."

I flash him my you-should-have-known-better look and turn off my iPad, setting it down on the sofa where he'll probably knock it off later by flopping down like an injured seal.

"Well, now you know. Variety isn't always the best thing for you."

Hint, hint. Keep a girl a little longer than a few hours, Von Bremen.

"I know that *now*, no thanks to you."

I ignore that cute little hate glare he has going on and, instead, offer him something I know will make him feel better.

"How 'bout I make your game-day cookies a little earlier so you can have two?"

Those navy eyes brighten with one word. Two. The boy *always* wants two cookies. What he gets: one cookie. Refined sugar is Theo's demon. And if he wasn't going to go run this off in a few hours, then I wouldn't give it to him. Theo after sugar is like driving on the autobahn. It's all fun and games until someone slows down.

"Okay, go shower and I'll make your cookies."

With a wary glance, Theo chugs the rest of his water and tosses the bottle in our recycling bin. "Promise?"

Have mercy.

"Yes, I promise, you can have two. Hurry so we can stretch your shoulder before you leave."

The man who kills bugs for me pops a ridiculous grin on his face. "Deal."

We're late.

It's all Theo's fault.

"I can't believe you had to stop by three stores to find your passion fruit bubble gum for game day," he teases sarcastically, shoving two pieces in his mouth.

My eyes roll at his blatant lie. We all know who needed the gum.

You don't come between a player and his game-day ritual. These guys have a strict superstition that must be followed. If he requires passion fruit bubble gum, then passion fruit gum he will get. Even if it does put us at the field ten minutes before first pitch.

"Go, weirdo, before Coach benches you. I'll lock up."

Gah, the grin he gives me is downright kissable.

"That's my girl."

He turns his cheek to the side, and if we had more time, I would aggravate him and ask if he needs anything else, but since we don't, I give in to another ritual and plant a good-luck kiss to his dimpled cheek.

"Go get 'em, Teddy."

"Ugh. Don't call me Teddy."

I'll call him anything I want. After all the years we've been friends, I have earned the right to call him Teddy.

"Fine. Go get 'em, T-Dog."

His face is one of horror.

"I take it back. Teddy is fine."

See? I knew he would come around.

I chuckle, snagging the keys from his hand.

"Remember, throw first-pitch strikes. You do better in the count when you throw a strike first."

He nods seriously.

"Hurry. Get out of here!"

Like he just remembered we're running behind, his eyes go wide, and he scrambles out of the car, yelling over his shoulder, "Sit where I can see you!"

Have mercy. This man....

Efficiently, I have my water and fold-up chair tucked underneath my arm. I need a free hand to lock Theo's old-ass car that has no key fob. When I get everything situated, finally, I jog up to the field, already sweating.

I don't bother with the bleachers and take my spot behind the fence, right behind home base where Theo can see me.

"Ms. McCallister." Frank, the umpire for tonight, nods at me with a stern look, also taking his spot behind the catcher.

I grin, unable to promise that I won't call him names or argue with his calls tonight. We both know how this goes down.

"Anniston!"

I turn at the familiar voice. A replica of Theo, Thad stands behind me with a big, stupid grin on his face. His hands are full with a tray of food and drinks.

"I have nachos." He waggles his brows, and it makes me laugh.

Grinning—and really excited for my nachos—I glance back at the mound, spotting Theo warming up. His gaze is fixed on me and Thad.

I wave awkwardly.

"Focus, Teddy!" I yell, not giving a fuck about using the nickname he hates so badly.

His cheek twitches, and very slowly, his stare tears away from the two of us.

"Watch my slider," he yells back from the mound, digging a hole by the plate using his cleat. "I keep missing the corner."

I nod, knowing he needs my help, and look back at Thad with a sad smile. "Start without me. I'll come when the inning is over."

Thad flashes me an understanding smile and nods, already heading into the stands.

I turn back to Theo.

"Okay, Von Bremen, paint me a corner."

A triumphant grin emerges, and it makes me smile.

"Come on, Frank! The tailgaters in the parking lot could see that was a strike!"

Frank ignores me for the two hundredth time this inning. Seriously, his eyesight is getting bad. Someone has to tell him.

I give Theo, who looks about ready to explode, our sign for a curve ball. I don't care what Brody, his catcher for today, is calling. Theo needs to get this guy to reach for the ball by throwing it closer to his hands. Theo's been pitching him down and outside, trying to get him to chase, but he's been smart. A curve ball will work.

Finally, Theo nods and goes into his wind up. I'm clenched, probably more anxious than Coach Anderson since Theo will lose his no-hitter if this guy hits the ball. Or worse, walks.

The crowd hushes, waiting on the pitch, when I hear a whispered voice in my ear.

"I polished off all the nachos. I rate them a 3.5 on our nacho scale."

Fuck.

I totally forgot about Thad being here, and I normally never forget nachos. With my gaze still focused on Theo, I whisper, "Just a 3.5?"

"Unfortunately."

"Sounds like you saved me some calories. How 'bout I make up for the shitty ballpark nachos with some of my famous pancakes?"

Thad's eyes light up at the mention of someone cooking for him. We go out to eat a lot. It's rare we have time to cook anymore.

"Absolutely," he agrees. "I'll bring beer."

I can't even laugh at the beer comment because Theo throws a pitch and it's straight down the middle. The batter doesn't miss, crushing Theo's no-hitter with one smooth swing, dropping the ball into the outfield with a double.

"Fuck!" Theo shouts behind his glove, glaring at me and Thad.

Thad chooses to ignore his brother's tantrum and continues our conversation as if he doesn't feel the daggers shooting from Theo's harsh gaze.

"I'll meet you both at the apartment. Is eight o'clock good?"

My smile wavers as Theo's no-hitter game is obliterated, just like his attitude.

I manage to hold my smile though. Thad can't help the fact Theo's pitch was off.

"Sounds like a plan. We'll see you later."

Apart from the one batter, Theo sits the rest of their team down one right after the other once Thad leaves. The Yellowjackets are once again the victors thanks to Theo's pitching skills.

Shifting my weight from one foot to the other, I wait for Theo to come out of the clubhouse. I'm not sure if he'll shower at school or go home. You can never tell when he's mad.

"You need a ride?"

I jerk at the voice behind me.

"Uh… no. I'm good," I tell the right fielder, Max. I don't know him really well, but he's always nice to me when we cross paths.

"You sure?"

He really is cute with his tan skin and dark hair. The dimple is probably what does it for me. It's deep just like Theo's.

"She's fucking sure."

Quickly Max's smile turns serious when he hears Theo's menacing voice behind me.

Uh-oh. A shower didn't settle him down.

I smile, not letting Theo's sour attitude piss all over Max's solid performance. "Thanks anyway, Max. You did good today, by the way."

Max keeps his focus on Theo but manages to tip his chin in my direction.

"Thanks, Ans—I mean, Anniston."

"Let's go," Theo barks, grabbing my elbow and pulling me toward the parking lot. I wave at Max and struggle to keep up with Theo's pace.

"Did you want to work on your curve ball?" I ask hesitantly.

He clips out a quick, "No," before unlocking the door and meeting my eyes over the top of the car. "You suck."

My mouth falls open. "I suck?" I swear my eyebrows are to my hairline. "Why do I suck?" Was I not the perfect cheerleader? Did I not coach him to a victory?

"You weren't paying attention. I lost my no-hitter."

Okay. I see how this is going to go down. Petty.

"Do not try and pin the one hit on me, Theo."

His glare never wavers, so I continue trying to talk sense into this man. "What are you going to do when this season is over and you're in Washington without me, huh?"

His jaw clenches and the precious dimple I love so much never appears. "You could come with me."

I sigh. We've talked about this.

"You know I can't."

"You can't or you won't?"

Maybe a little of both.

"You know I want to go to med school here in Georgia," I counter.

He scoffs, taking off his hat and running his fingers through his hair. "Washington has good schools too."

I'm sure they do, but when Theo decided he wanted to go pro

with his baseball career, I knew I would always come second. I knew we would be separated eventually, and as the last month of our senior year ticks away, both of us are feeling a little insecure. We've always had each other.

"Let's not talk about this right now, okay?" I attempt a smile. "Let's celebrate your win instead."

It takes him a minute, but eventually he agrees and comes around to unlock my door like a gentleman.

"I told Brody we'd make an appearance at his party tonight."

Ugh.

"Sounds fun! I just need to text Thad. I promised him dinner."

Theo slams his door harder than necessary.

"He'll live."

Chapter Four

Theo

I'm a bastard.

Especially on days that end in Y.

It's a well-known fact humans like to point blame. Me especially. So the fact that I'm a bastard really boils down to two root causes. Or people. Same difference.

Anniston McCallister and yours truly.

One could argue Anniston is simply an innocent bystander in all of this, but I'm not that *one,* and Anniston—no matter how much she would like people to believe—is not innocent.

She's not.

Anniston McAllister showed me early on in life that everything is temporary.

Life is temporary.

Girlfriends are temporary.

Bad seasons are temporary.

The point is, I knew before she insulted me, my relationship with her would be temporary.

She is beautiful, smart, and for some unknown reason, wants to be my friend.

Good shit like that doesn't last long for people like me—to bastards like me. People like me are angry motherfuckers. Sporadic and irrational are the founding traits of our personality.

It's science, or maybe it's the whole nature versus nurture thing? Or maybe it's because I'm a greedy asshole and I took what I didn't deserve.

You grow up knowing everything is shared when you have a sibling your own age. You learn to be clever and react quickly when something catches your eye.

In this case, I knew from the moment I saw Anniston McCallister that I wanted her.

Really. Fucking. Bad.

I wasn't sharing her, and I sure as fuck wasn't doing temporary with her.

So I became ruthless.

I charged my way through every boy who dared flash a smile in her direction, including my brother.

She was mine. All fucking mine.

Where I went wrong in this quest for permanence was growing complacent. I grew comfortable as I obliterated every dick out of her life. Spending time with her became easy...

Until now.

Until I'm left with four fucking weeks.

And I want every goddamned minute of them.

So fuck Thad and his stupid nachos and ridiculous shorts.

Fuck his and Anniston's friendship.

And fuck him for stealing even forty-five seconds of my time left with her.

I know that sounds trivial and petty, and sure, I should be less upset about losing less than a minute of Anniston's attention and more upset over the mediocrity of my performance, but I'm not. I'm man enough to admit I'm being an asshole about something stupid.

But you don't understand.

Anniston McCallister behind the plate is like not washing my socks before game day. It's a must-have or everything turns to shit.

The fact is, I can't remember a time when I haven't seen those blue eyes shining in excitement through the fence. Let me put it in perspective for you: having Anniston's sole attention feels like what I imagine standing on the mound in game seven of the World Series with your last pitch deciding the fate of the championship. The hope in the fans' eyes as they stand, cheering for you, rooting for you to reach deep within your soul and channel every ounce of power into one solitary pitch.

That's what it feels like when Anniston's eyes are on me.

It's that moment Thad took from me.

So call me needy, call me a diva, I really don't give a fuck.

I've grown accustomed to Anniston's attention and maybe even… her love. Either way, I can no longer live without it. And as the days draw nearer to my departure, I should feel anything other than angry. I should be happy. I'm finally leaving this small town and getting out from under my father's business. But I'm not happy. Because each game, each practice, is a countdown to losing my constant. My biggest fan. My girl.

Who is going to stare at me from behind the net when I'm in Washington? Who will call the pitches they know I can throw? Who will inspire me to dig deep, fight the feeling of failure, and chase my dreams?

No one! That's fucking who!

Because the only person in my life who inspires these feelings is staying right. Fucking. Here. In Madison. With my brother—*let's not forget that little tidbit*—and the other thousands of men I warded off for the last seven years.

I'm leaving her alone, unprotected from the hound dogs of central Georgia.

And it crushes my soul.

To the extent I can't sleep. I barely eat—unless she cooks for me, let's not get too dramatic. All I can do is think about leaving her behind.

For someone else to love her.

To steal her away.

Seeing her standing there behind the fence, blonde hair falling out of my hat, was just like staring back at the fourteen-year-old girl who showed up to my game for the first time all those years ago. I'd found myself in the middle of a tied game with a full count and twitchy hitter. I remember wiping the sweat from my brow and rubbing the ball in my hands until my breaths evened out. There was no point looking into the stands for support. My parents had never come to any of my games. They had better things to do than sweat and watch their son sling a ball around in the dirt.

I'd grown accustomed to pitching to a faceless crowd. I'd grown tired of the game with each throw. What was the point? At first, baseball was something I loved. Later it became an escape.

Standing on that mound in ninth grade? It had become a chore. I was bored.

Baseball was routine, nothing like it used to be when me and my dad would spend the evenings in the front yard tossing the ball around.

So I pissed the talent away with my moods.

Until I heard her voice.

"Stop fucking around, Von Bremen, and finish this!"

I remember my head snapping up, locating that voice I talked to every night on the phone. Anniston McCallister had become the constant in my life. Someone I looked forward to seeing every holiday when I could return home.

The girl I had spent my whole summer laughing and arguing with stood on the bleachers, blocking several parents' view, with her hands cupped around her mouth.

She was beautiful.

She was loud.

And she was at my school.

At my game.

Wearing my number with what looked like a homemade shirt.

And she dropped an F-bomb that sent collective gasps all around the bleachers.

I was so goddamned proud in that moment I could have volunteered somewhere stupid with Thad.

And then she went and raised those scrawny arms in the air like she was silently asking me what the fuck I was doing.

I was done.

Then and fucking there.

And then she gave me the sign. I only knew two pitches back then, and she knew one was better than the other.

She gave me the sign for the curve.

And when I threw it—perfectly on the corner—her arms went up and her scream deafened all of the uppity women next to her.

But it wasn't that moment that sealed Anniston's fate.

It wasn't her smile either.

Nope.

It was when she jumped on those silver benches, turning around to high-five her grandfather, that I knew she was mine.

Because she told me in thick black tape that stretched across her back, spelling out my name.

Von Bremen.

It was the first shirt of many she would wear to my games after I packed my shit and threatened my father with failing grades if he didn't let me attend Anniston's school. It was low and immature but was exactly what I needed. My constant.

So again, really, today's outburst is all Anniston's fault.

She made me greedy.

She made me want it all.

And Thad got in the way of my peace.

"Don't you have something better to do tonight than hang out at a baseball party?" I hold back a glare, picking at the label on Anniston's lotion. After the game, we stopped by the house so Ans could shower Thad's breath off of her. Okay, fine. It was dirt.

"Anniston invited me."

Of course she did. She's a bleeding fucking heart.

"Why? Do you not want me to come?"

I almost groan and roll my eyes, but I don't because Thad Von Bremen would think he still has a shot with my girl. And he doesn't. Just because I haven't asked her out yet, does not mean she's available. It's an unwritten rule.

"You can come. I was just curious," I lie. "I figured you might have a date with Sheila."

My brother's eyes go squinty. "Her name is Sasha, and she has a study session tonight."

Ah, the smart girls. They always have their priorities fucked up.

"Don't look at me like that. I *do* get laid, Theo."

No, he doesn't. Otherwise he would be at this "study session" with Sonya, fingering her under the table when she answered a question right. Instead, he's third-wheeling it with me and Anniston by attending a victory party.

"I didn't say anything." I laugh, amused at his crimson cheeks. See? No pussy for Thaddeus Von Bremen.

"At least I *have* a girlfriend," he counters, acting like that's a trophy-worthy statement.

It's not.

"Having a girlfriend is like—" I take a breath and look at the ceiling as if I'm searching for some profound words. "—having a puppy." I bite my lip, containing my grin and hold up one finger. With as much seriousness as I can manage, I rattle off, "You have to feed them premium, organic food or they will get a stomachache and vomit."

Thad rolls his eyes, but I keep going, holding up the second finger.

"If you don't take them out or give 'em attention, they whine." Another finger.

"Their grooming will cost you a small fortune."

I start to make my last point, but a hand covers my fingers, pushing them down.

"But if you stroke them just right, they might lick your fingers and play with your balls."

Thad coughs.

But me? I smile so big my fucking cheeks hurt.

Did I not say Anniston was my girl?

I slide off the barstool and turn, facing a grinning and freshly showered Ans.

"Are you saying you want a dog, McCallister?"

She shrugs, taking a sip of my beer without asking. "I could go for something humping my leg every now and again."

This time it's Thad who laughs and me who chokes.

The fuck? She wants someone to hump her?

Her comment grounds me to reality.

Anniston is going to move on. She's going to find a dude to hump her.

"Are you finally ready or do we need to wait a million more years?" I snap, my asshole back intact and ready to make people cry tonight.

"Come on, Teddy, just because you're a pussy kind of guy doesn't mean you have to hate on us dog lovers."

Don't lay her over this island, Theo. Don't rip those shorts down her legs and spank the fucking sass out of her. Not tonight, dude.

Not. Tonight.

"That was cringy," I lie. "I hope you aren't planning to crack awkward jokes tonight."

I shudder, and it causes her to throw her head back and polish off my beer before breezing past me and throwing over her shoulder, "Find some pussy tonight, Von Bremen. You seem pent up."

If glaring was in the Guinness World Records, I would hold the number one spot. "I'm not pent up. You took forever in the bathroom and now I'm tired."

And horny.

But that's beside the fact.

"Stay here," she suggests, slipping on her sandals by the door.

She's crazy if she thinks that's happening.

"Yeah, bro," Thad adds, like he wants me to push him down the stairs. "Stay here and rest. I'll look after Ans tonight."

Mom will miss him, but she'll eventually move on, right?

Ugh.

I look at Thad and then at a grinning Anniston before I kill the mood completely.

"The only rest I plan on doing is between transferring my dick from a mouth to a pussy. Now get in the fucking car before I leave both of you."

Unfortunately, my mood hasn't improved since we left and drove here in silence. I considered apologizing but thought better of it.

Anniston baited me and so did Thad. I reacted like I always do. Like an ass.

"Good game, Theo," some girl coos in my ear, her breath smelling like cheap beer and mint gum.

It does nothing for me.

"Thanks," I say flatly, taking a drink of the disgusting beer someone shoved in my hand as soon as I got here. Anniston took off about half an hour ago when my teammates pushed me out the door and onto the back patio where they were set up around a chimenea.

I didn't want to join them. Frankly, I would rather let Wendy with the fat hands finger my asshole.

But I'm supposed to participate, because teams that have a strong bond win games.

I think it's total bullshit.

Winning teams are because of hard work, not because we fart around and have a beer under the stars.

"Are you always that serious on the mound?"

Is she still fucking here?

"He's always serious," chimes Brody, my catcher and best friend. "Only McCallister can charm the devil into smiling."

Was my best friend.

"Ha!" I say, unamused before flipping him off.

"Who's McCallister?"

The girl who had been lurking behind my back finally grows enough balls to come stand in front of me, working her way in between my legs.

Any other night, I would be relieved I didn't have to charm a girl into my pants. This one made it easy. She's not ugly. Her hair is down and wavy in a way that looks messed. Jeans with more holes than fabric cling to her toned thighs, and I can totally see a camel toe. Pair that with a sweet, rounded face that her daddy is probably proud of, and you get a decent, hometown girl, whom I will more than likely fuck before the night is over.

"Don't worry about it," I say, opening my legs wider so she can sit on my lap. She needs no more invitation from me.

"I'm Monica," she chirps out with far too much enthusiasm.

I look at Brody who grins, darting his eyes to the patio doors.

The fucker does it on purpose. He knows I have to look.

Hell, I haven't stopped looking.

Anniston fucking McCallister in her barely there tank top is set up at the beer pong table with Thad and another guy I don't know.

"Who the fuck is that guy?" I ask Brody, straightening my spine and moving Monica out of my line of sight. Brody purposely hesitates to get on my last damn nerve. "Don't fuck with me. Who is he?"

He chuckles. "Bo. He's new. Just transferred from Savannah State."

What kind of name is Bo? The dead kind if he grabs her again. I don't give a shit she is wiping the floor with these douches in beer pong. She could easily win in any other game as well. Anniston is a natural athlete. If she plays something, you better know she aims to win it.

"I heard he's quite curious about your roommate."

He's baiting me. I know this, but somehow I can't help but to respond.

"I hope you told him about Anniston's crazy fetish with diaper bondage."

44

Monica shifts on my lap and makes a noise like she needs attention or be pushed off.

"I didn't, but I figured you'd prefer to warn him in person like you do everyone."

How thoughtful.

"Bo is prelaw," he adds. "He's finishing his senior year at Berkshire."

Poor Monica doesn't get a warning. At Brody's admission, I jump up, sending Monica down in a tangle of arms and skinny jeans.

"Anniston's Berkshire?"

His nod is slow and amused.

"Yep."

Fuck me.

Looks like Ans might get her wish. After all, Bo is a dog's name.

Chapter Five

Anniston

B o is a terrible beer pong partner. So bad, I want to ask him to feign injury and gracefully retire to the sofa so Thad and I can kick some ass like we always do at these boring-ass parties. You would think baseball players would know how to party, but they don't. Football players on the other hand…

"Your turn, cutie," he interrupts.

If I didn't mention it before, Bo is also horrible at nicknames.

Apart from those two things, though, he isn't so bad. He's handsome with his surfer good looks and endearing southern charm. His hair looks like it's in a perpetual state of chaos, and I've yet to see him frown.

I smile easy, letting the nickname thing go, and turn to face the table.

"If you bounce the ball hard to the left, I think you could get the cup on the edge," Thad whispers in my ear.

Instead of being my cheerleader like Bo, Thad knows exactly what kind of talk I desire in the middle of a ridiculous game. I'm not like other girls, so his strategy talk turns my smile into something more genuine. With no need to clarify, I flick my wrist and release the ball just how Thad instructed. The ball bounces right into the red solo cup, making a plopping noise.

"Drink up, boys." I laugh. "Hell, I might even drink with you."

I eye the several full cups on our side of the net. "From the way this game is panning out, I might end up being the DD tonight."

Theo's teammates groan but take it like the men they aren't and designate the rookie to down the cheap alcohol in the cup the ball landed.

"So… do you go to Cantor," Bo asks, leaning against the table while the guys chant for the rookie to "chug."

Thad makes an amused noise that I ignore.

"No, I attend Berkshire."

Bo's eyebrows lift. "Oh. How about that? I do too."

How unfortunate.

I flash him a smile like I'm impressed. Truth is, I've been attracted to dozens of guys at school, but it doesn't matter. Because none of them knot my stomach like the man I go home to every night.

With fake enthusiasm, I return, "What a coincidence."

Thad resumes the game by taking his turn, ringing yet another cup and making the baseball team look like little league players.

"Do you stay on campus?"

Oh, jeez. Here we go. Let it go, dude. I'm not interested.

"Uh, no. I live with my roommate."

And he will make you cry if you show up at our apartment. He's considerate like that.

"Oh really? Does she go to Berkshire too?"

"He goes to Cantor," comes Thad's voice. "Your turn."

Bo's expression goes from excited to confused in a second. "He?"

Sigh. *Yes, Bo. He. As in male. As in he carries a Y chromosome.*

Thad grows exasperated as Bo ruins the fun of the game for him. "Anniston and my brother have lived together for four years." Thad gives Bo this look I can't quite make out.

"Oh."

Yeah, oh. We're complicated, Bo. Some would even say we're stupid for not being together. It's not like I haven't tried to incentivize Von Bremen to take the leap into relationship territory, but somehow the timing is always off.

Truth be told, we're scared. We've been through so much. What if we take this step and destroy the only good relationship we have?

Yeah, it's a fine line. And we walk it every single day.

I chance a look through the glass doors leading out to the patio and see Theo glaring at me. A girl with chestnut hair is wrapped around him, playing with the curls sticking out of the bottom of his hat.

My curls.

Immediately I sober, glaring right back at the man I'm riding home with. Maybe. I might decide to ride home with someone else now.

"So are you two like… together?"

Bo is not letting this go. Good. I could use a distraction since Theo is obviously celebrating without me.

"No, we're just friends," I grit out before turning around and flashing him a fake smile.

Friends. Fucking friends.

Ugh.

Bo grins, and it's easy and extremely cute. "Good. Just friends is great."

Is it, Bo? Really?

I try not to frown and agree like I'm supposed to. "Yep."

Back in the game, Bo extends his hand to me, the pong ball elevated in his fingers. "Blow and give me good luck."

And this is why Bo and I would never work.

Skill and luck are two separate things. We aren't at a wishing well here. We are playing a game. A game that requires skill. A skill Thad and I have and Bo lacks. Blowing on his fucking ball is not going to help any of us.

But the hope and innocence on his face makes me feel like shit, so I do it anyway.

"Maybe I'll just keep this ball instead?" he teases.

Ugh. Yeah, see? No, this will not work, but before I can respond my phone buzzes in my pocket.

Theo: This isn't Vegas. Douche doesn't need you spitting on his ball. He already sucks enough.

This motherfucker.

How dare he insult me for blowing on the boy's ball for luck?

Anniston: This isn't a pay by the hour motel. You and Monica need to take your horrible manners to a back room and not where everyone can witness your tasteless attraction.

I watch as he reads my message, a slow grin pulling across his face. A second later, another text dings.

Theo: Her name is Martha, and she's giving me tips on deep conditioning my hair.

He's fucking with me and trying to make me laugh. It's not going to work this time.

Anniston: Her name is Monica, and she's a Poli Sci major. Take it somewhere else.

I start to tuck my phone away when a terrible wave of pettiness hits me, and I send one more.

Anniston: Like I'm about to.

With one last smirk in Theo's direction, I tuck my phone away and turn to the table, intent on ignoring him for the rest of the evening. Let him have a blast with Monica or Martha, or whatever he wants to call her.

"Is it my turn again?" I ask the guys. Thad nods, taking a sip of his own beer, since apparently the drunken baseball players won't be able to score.

Good. I take the ball, eyeing the last cup on the right side and take a deep breath.

You got this, Anniston. Let it all go. Let the fact you got up at 5:00 a.m. this morning to run with Theo before you massaged his shoulder until your hand cramped so bad you had to ice it.

Let go of the fact you made him a protein shake and stayed up late watching game footage until you fell asleep, taking notes of his competitors' weaknesses just so he would be ready for tonight's game.

Let go that he will probably make you bum a ride so he can go back to Monica's and get a victory blowie on her pink bedspread.

Let it go that he doesn't want to celebrate his win with you.

With one last breath, I release the ball and it bounces with grace and lands dead center into the last cup.

Thad whoops the loudest, but it's Bo that shocks me the most by lifting me in his arms and swinging me around.

"You are a beast!" he praises, his laughter overshadowing the groans of the baseball team.

I find myself laughing as he twirls me around and around until a sharp sting to my leg stops us both.

"Oh, shit. I'm so sorry."

Bo places me on my feet and squats down to look at my leg where he banged it on the edge of the ping pong table.

"It's okay." I wave him off. "I'll be fine."

His eyes narrow, and his hand hesitates at my leg as if he's contemplating touching me.

"You're bleeding."

I look down and, sure enough, I am.

"It's just a scratch," I argue. "I'll clean it up in the bathroom."

Bo, being the chivalrous southerner, isn't having it. "Come on, my friend lives here. I'm sure he has bandages somewhere."

Before I can argue, I'm being pulled up the stairs and into some dude's room. It's clean-ish. His clothes are scattered around the floor like makeshift rugs to cover the million stains on the carpet, but the bed is made and that surprises me the most.

"Stay here. I'll check the bathroom for a first aid kit."

Bo flashes me a genuine smile before he taps the doorframe and darts off to save the day. You have to give it to him, even if he is a terrible beer pong player; he's a really sweet guy. Maybe I shouldn't be so quick to discount him as a potential boyfriend. I mean, what if Theo and I never become more than friends? What if Bo turns into the next millionaire, and I end up having to go on a reality show to find a man?

"I promise not to move," I tell him, making myself comfortable on a stranger's bed.

Bo nods, and it's the flicker in his gaze that has me swallowing past a sudden knot in my throat.

Don't complicate things for me, Bo. I'm not sure I can handle it. I've lived my entire teen years knowing exactly who I want. I can't afford to crush those fantasies yet. I might not survive it.

While I wait for Bo to return, I chance the risk of catching an incurable disease and lie back on what I hope is a clean quilt.

"I'm not helping you raise another man's baby, just so you know."

The sound of his voice has me shooting upright.

Casually leaning against the frame of the door is the man who let me pee in his Yeti cup when I refused to squat in the woods when we camped for the first and last time. There were snakes, okay? I'm not that outdoorsy.

Fighting back a grin, I counter, "Who says we won't live happily ever after?"

His eyes roll, but he doesn't move from his position. "How many times do I have to tell you, McCallister? A wet hole is a wet hole to these guys. Unless love is a metaphorical term for a condom, it doesn't come into play during sex."

His words are biting, and they chip away at the edges of my heart, but I remain unaffected. This is his way of pushing everyone away. Except me. I'm stronger than he thinks. I'm still here, rooted firmly to the ground.

"Are those the sweet words you used to lure Monica into a dark closet?"

I really don't want to know, but I can't help myself.

He smirks.

"Mavis required zero effort on my part. I could have just unzipped my pants and she would have face planted into my crotch."

Vulgar and crass. Another deterrent from the actual truth. But he said, "could have." He *could have* unzipped his pants, but he didn't, and that makes me all kinds of excited.

"Monica sounds like a rare gem," I muse too happily.

Theo grunts. "Where's your little lap dog?"

His raspy voice shouldn't make me want to fuck with him, but that's exactly what I do.

"He needed to grab something from the bathroom." I shrug. Let Theo assume Bo went to get a condom.

Theo's eyes narrow into slits right at the time Bo's excited voice carries down the hallway. "Found one!"

At the sound of Bo's footsteps, Theo pushes off the doorframe and stands in the center, causing Bo to run into his hulking body.

"Oomph. Uh…?"

Theo rights poor Bo and pats him on the chest. Bo looks at me over his shoulder, his forehead creased in the middle. "Sorry, I didn't—"

Theo plucks the bandage from his fingers and examines it without a word.

"What the fuck is this?" he asks Bo with incredulity.

"A bandage?" Bo sounds unsure, and it makes me laugh. Theo has that effect on people.

"Why do you have a bandage?"

Apparently Theo needs it broken down for him.

"Anniston, she uh…" Bo runs his hands through his hair, and Theo decides he's done trying to pull answers from someone who can't form complete sentences.

"Why do you need a fucking bandage, Ans?" His stare is fierce as his eyes roam up and down my body, looking for the injury and finally noticing my leg. He rushes in and kneels in front of me, his fingers softly probing the tender skin on my shin.

"It's just a scratch," I offer, but Bo decides to be Honest Abe and piss Theo off even more.

"I accidentally swung her into the table."

Theo's hand tightens around my leg, and I quickly distract him by lifting his chin so he can look at me, but it doesn't matter because the asshole has already been unleashed.

"I can take it from here," he grounds out, surprising me. That wasn't too asshole.

With one last look at Bo, I offer a smile. "See ya later, Bo. Thanks for the bandage."

No use in promising to see him again. We both know I won't.

His smile is weak, but he nods in return. "Maybe we'll see each other on campus."

Theo's hand spasms against my skin, and I know for Bo's safety he should probably go.

"Hopefully," I say, praying he takes the hint.

Theo decides enough is enough and jumps in. "Hopefully you won't make her bleed the next time you see her."

Oh hell.

With that, Bo leaves. I push at Theo's shoulder.

"It's a fucking scratch, not malaria. What's your deal?"

He doesn't look at me. Instead, he opens the wrapped bandage and proceeds to gently cover the wound. "You made me believe you and he were about to have sex," he accuses, never meeting my eyes.

"And? What if we were?"

He softly presses the adhesive to my skin before lowering his head and placing a kiss to the edge. A tingle shoots down my spine, and I stifle a gasp, reaching for his head, still covered with a cap. How I want to snatch it off and run my fingers through his hair…

With his eyes still on my leg, he sits upright, his hands rubbing up my thighs and stopping at the hem of my shorts. My breath catches in my throat. This is it. This is when he makes his move.

Except, he stops. His fingers halt their advance as his chest rises and falls harshly.

"Theo," I whisper between us.

His chest rumbles and a groan fills the quiet space, and his head lowers again, this time hovering over my center. Lower, he inches down until his nose is nearly pushed in between my thighs. My breath is choppy and harsh as I wait to see what he does next as his fingers tighten, holding me close.

"Mmm…," he hums, the sexy sound vibrating between my legs and sending chills along my arms.

And then his mouth descends on me, his wet tongue licking the muscle of my thigh right before he…

"Ow!" I cry out, shoving a laughing Theo away. "What the fuck?" I rub the blooming red mark. "Why did you bite me, asshole?"

His expression is a mixture of smug and pissed.

"Come on, I'm ready to go. This party fucking sucks."

Chapter Six

Theo

I could smell her. An alluring exotic flavor specifically tailored to my taste. Anniston McCallister had me aching in my jeans. Fucking aching. I was so close… So close to just giving in to the selfish part of me and taking what I wanted.

Her.

But I didn't. Thad would be proud.

"What do you mean, this party sucks? You're the one who wanted to come."

I can't tell her I couldn't focus after seeing her being pulled up the stairs like a sacrificial lamb. I shoved Monica into Brody faster than she could promise me a lackluster blow job.

Nothing was stopping me from snatching Anniston's ass off some flea-ridden bed and tossing her into my car. Hines would be appalled at her behavior.

And it was all for a motherfucking bandage.

This clumsy dipshit knocked her glorious legs into the damn table… what an idiot.

"I didn't want to come," I say, grabbing Anniston's hand and tugging her behind me. "I was obligated to come. And I did." I shrug. "Now we can leave."

I pull us through the mass of sweaty bodies and hold my breath. Deodorant apparently comes at a premium at this party.

"What about Thad?"

God-fucking-dammit.

I throw my head back, done with this fucking night already.

Reluctantly, I let her hand go to grab my phone and find my fucking brother who she just had to invite.

"There he is," she shouts, saving me the trouble of calling him.

Cupping my hands on each side of my mouth, I shout over the heads of the people in my way.

"Thad! Let's go, fucker, or I'm leaving you."

Thad's head lifts from the guy he's talking to. He sees my face and then glances back at Anniston.

What the actual fuck?

"Are you coming or what?"

It wouldn't be too awful if I just left him, right?

"I'll get a ride from Brody," he yells in return.

Finally something goes right.

I nod in return and grab Anniston's hand, reaching the car faster than she can see clumsy-ass Bo watching her with something like desire from the corner.

I get her buckled in and trot around the front of the car before getting in and sighing with something like relief.

She gives me a minute before she says, "You okay to drive?"

I cut her a look. Does she honestly think I would risk her life and mine by driving drunk?

"I'm fine. I only had one beer."

She shrugs. "Just checking."

We drive in silence after that. Neither of us bother turning the radio on or filling the silence with talking. It isn't until I pull into the parking lot of the stadium that she speaks.

"You want to work on a pitch?"

Everything in me wants to pop off with something asshole, but I hold back because that's not why I brought her to the baseball field.

"Come on," I tell her softly.

She follows, completely trusting. I take her hand again, and when we get to the locked gate of the field, I tip my chin. We're going to have to climb over. The few security lights are still on, so it won't be a big deal. The outer fence is only four foot. Anniston and I have climbed taller fences in the dark before.

I climb over first and offer my hand to help her over, which she doesn't accept.

"What are we doing, Theo?"

Yes, what are *we doing, Theo?*

"Race me."

Her hearty laugh makes me smile.

"You're serious?" she says, already slipping off her sandals.

That's my girl... She never turns down a competition.

"Is it your ADHD? You need to run it out?"

It would be so easy to just agree and not make her think this is anything but just wanting to spend time with her on the ball field under the stars.

Rather than answer her, I deflect. "Are you scared I might beat you, McCallister?"

At my challenge, her smile turns into something devious. "I'm never scared, Von Bremen."

I swallow. *She's* never scared, but I am.

Shrugging off that voice that is nagging me to tell her how I really feel, I make my way to home plate and raise my brows. "Are you coming?"

At my comment, she hurries to my side. Facing the first base bag, both of us ready into a crouch.

"On the count of three…"

Anniston nods her agreement, and I count down. "One…two…"

At "three" we both take off. Anniston is several steps ahead of me. I'm no loser though, so I put all my weight forward before lunging and tackling her to the ground at shortstop.

"Theo!" she hollers in between laughter. "You are such a sore loser!"

Or an opportunist. I can see it both ways.

I make sure I roll us around, reddening her blonde hair with the infield's red dirt. She's squealing, fighting my hold as the air grows dusty around us.

"I'm getting filthy," she cries in my arms.

Not filthy enough, but I don't say that.

"You're not becoming a girl on me, are you?"

It's a stupid thing to say because she stops laughing. "I've always been a girl, Theo."

I stop rolling, hovering over her in the dirt. "I fucking know," I growl.

Seriously, I jerked off every day I got home from school. Some would say that's normal for a teenage boy, but when you have to do it every time after seeing her, it gets a little weird.

Sighing, Anniston shoves me off, and I lie beside her, both of us staring at the clear skies.

After a moment, when we both have settled down, she speaks. "Are you scared?"

It feels like I've been shot. My chest spasms and fear creeps up my spine when I answer, dreading her response. "About what?"

A pregnant pause hangs between when she finally responds. "About moving. About leaving Georgia…"

I clear my throat, buying time. The truth is, I could give two shits about leaving Georgia. I care about leaving her, which is why I do this dance with her on a daily basis.

About a year ago, I had acted shitty when some frat boy showed up at our door intending on taking Anniston out. She happened to still be at school, but Thad was there, and he witnessed me ripping up Dude's number and flushing it down the toilet.

I hadn't felt bad about it at all. Anniston didn't need to go out with this dude. He was wearing tennis shorts for heaven's sake. Tennis. Shorts. Let that sink in for a moment. Does Anniston strike you as someone who could hang at a country club? The girl drops way too many F-bombs. She would have embarrassed that little piece of man meat before they even ordered the main course.

I thought I was doing her a favor.

Thad disagreed.

"You need to shit or get off the pot," he had said to me as I watched the ripped pieces of paper circle the bowl Anniston had just cleaned that morning.

"I don't know what you mean. Is that some new millennial term I don't know about?"

Thad looked at me accusingly before he said the words that would forever haunt me. "You're leaving. You're not ready to settle down. Don't string her along and ask her to wait for you while you plow through half the country living it up in the minor leagues. Let her go, Theo. For once in your life, think about someone other than yourself. Let her go."

It was hard not to throat punch him. He had a point. I was leaving, and she was staying here. Without me.

But he had a point. I wasn't ready to settle down, and it wasn't fair to drag Anniston along for the ride until I got my shit together.

So after a few sleepless nights, I decided Thad was right. I was being selfish with her. I expected her to wait for me, to be there for me as I chased my dreams. I needed to let her go and let her chase hers. Even without me.

It isn't something I want to do.

It isn't even something I'm good at doing.

I try though, and I think that should count for something.

Anniston's hand nudges me, reminding me I haven't answered her question. Taking her hand and interlacing our fingers, I decide to be honest for once.

"I'm not scared, but I'm worried about being so far away from you. What if you run out of toilet paper and don't have me to yell for?"

My joke lightens the heaviness on my chest until she rolls over, climbing on top of me in a straddle. Dust falls from her tangled hair and joins the red smudge on her cheek. She looks like a wild mess, and it's sexy as fuck.

"What are you going to do when you need someone to hold your hand when you have to get a flu shot every year? You think one of the players will let you cry on their shoulder?"

My eyes go squinty, and I try not to encourage her by laughing. "I did not cry."

She laughs. "Okay, you whimpered. Same difference."

Remember how I said I was an opportunist? Yeah, this is exhibit A.

I wrap my arms around her, enjoying the feel of her in my arms, and flip her onto her back. I pin her arms above her head and inch down so I'm in her face and her eyes are sparkling in the security light.

"McCallister," I say on a breath, "we both know you are higher maintenance than I am."

Total lie, but I can't very well admit that, now can I?

Her chest vibrates with a hearty laughter that reaches down into my soul and stays there, pulling up a chair and making itself comfortable.

"Whatever you say, Von Bremen. But…" She hesitates and sucks her bottom lip in between her teeth before closing her eyes so I can't see them get watery.

"But I will miss coaching you. God knows you need it."

At her last comment, she grins, and I fight the urge to beg her once more to come with me to Washington. Instead, I tickle her until we're both too tired to talk anymore.

Ans: I NEED YOU! EMERGENCY!

I look at the clock on the wall. Thirty minutes are left in the lecture. My fingers tap my phone screen. If I open the text and read it, she'll see and text me about three hundred more times. Professor Jenkins will inevitably need to see me after class about my lack of focus.

She can wait thirty minutes.

Ans: PLEASE, TEDDY!!!!!

Goddammit.

Theo: What's wrong?

Ans: All the girls are gone…

Ans: They totally wouldn't help me anyway.

Theo: Just tell me!

Ans: You were right.

It takes me a minute to analyze what she means. I was right? What did I say recently?

Ans: My pants are ruined!

Oh. *Oh.*

Motherfucker.

Theo: I'm not doing this again. You're fine. I'm sure you can make it home.

I put down my phone and try to focus on what Professor Jenkins is talking about. So far it sounds like a whole lot of shit I will never use.

Ans: It looks like a fucking crime scene, Theo! I can't make it home!

Ans: I neeeeeeeed you!

Sighing, I run my hands through my hair.

"Ugh." I nudge Brody's elbow. "I gotta get going. Can you take notes for me?"

He nods slowly, whispering, "You all right?"

I make a face like he just asked me if I grew a vagina over the Christmas holidays.

"I'm fine. Anniston needs me."

His grin is slow and stupid before he mouths, "Pussy whipped."

I wish. Her pussy is one thing I don't own.

With a slide of my hand, I knock his notebook off the ledge, sending his papers scattering. He scrambles to retrieve them, and I use the distraction to grab my shit and slip out.

As soon as I'm in the car, I call her. She answers immediately.

"I told ya, you were being bitchy this morning," I say as a way of greeting. She makes a noise in her throat that's half a laugh and half a scoff.

"Are we talking Super Plus then?" I continue, starting the car and backing out of my spot.

Her laugh brings a smile to my face.

"You're an ass."

"An ass you apparently need." I say "need" all whiny like she does when she's trying to talk me into something I don't want to do... like leaving class to buy tampons.

"What's my reward for saving the day?"

She knows I would have helped her anyway, but I like to make her come off something too.

She hums on the other end of the phone, her voice soft and quiet. "What do you want?"

Anything.

"Pancakes and Netflix."

She laughs. "You want to slum it, Von Bremen?"

Yep. That's exactly what I want to do today. If she's going to drag me out of class, then I'm damn sure not coming back for my afternoon class or practice. They can all just get over it.

"That's exactly what I want, McCallister. Do we have a deal?"

It's as if I can feel her smile when she says, "Deal."

The girl working the register has blown me a few times.

Maybe more.

Her face seems familiar, but her name escapes me.

"Will this be all?" she says sweetly, her voice dripping with a sexy rasp that gets me every fucking time.

Except today.

I have bigger excitement today than what's-her-name's wide jaw.

"Yep," I clip out, fishing a twenty out of my wallet and handing it over.

If she is wondering why I'm buying tampons, she doesn't ask. Most women who deal with me don't. I think they all know about mine and Anniston's relationship. Whatever it may be.

She hands me the change and slides the bag toward me. The name tag displays her name as Nan. Huh. I didn't peg her for a Nan.

I smile, avoiding her hand still clutching the bag. "Thanks. See ya around."

Instead of being subtle, she just goes for it. "Call me sometime. I've missed you."

Yeah… probably not going to happen.

I've significantly decreased my fuck sessions here recently.

Why? Well, if I'm going to be forced to cuddle, then I'd rather do it with the pretty little blonde that sleeps with her door cracked so I can watch her get off while she watches silly rom-com movies.

I make a noncommittal sound I hope she takes for a no and head out.

I make one more stop at the house before I pull up to the school and park by the gym's entrance where Anniston awaits.

Grabbing the bags, I strut into the elaborate gym that produces no pro athletes from its walls and find the girls' locker room, shouting, "Cover up, ladies! Guy coming in!"

After a moment, no one screams and I push through.

Chapter Seven

Anniston

I hear him before I see him.

My asshole hero.

Grinning, I step out of the shower room, securing the towel around me and pad out into the area where he's standing like he owns the room with his gym bag over his shoulder.

"Good evening, ma'am. I was dispatched to clean up a crime scene. Can you escort me to the area?"

This motherfucker wants me to marry him one day.

His stupid grin has the dimple in his cheek dipping low as if it wants me to lick it.

Not today, little dimple. Not yet.

Moving toward the man who ditched class to come to my rescue, I wrap my damp body around him and squeeze.

"Thank you, Teddy."

"Yeah, yeah," he says like he's annoyed, but he squeezes me back, so I know he's not that upset about leaving school or going to the drug store.

It was poor planning on my part. Usually I keep spare tampons in my bag, but I changed bags last night and I left it out. I also had one more damn day before I was supposed to start! I hate when my period is early.

"Here," he says, pulling back and sliding his gym bag over his shoulder. "I figured you needed clothes too."

I didn't, but I'm not going to tell him that.

Instead, I smile and kiss that fucking dimple. "You're the sweetest boy ever."

He's not a boy. He's all man. But when he looks shy and awkward, it makes me think of that little boy who would give me his jacket when I forgot mine.

"Let's not repeat that statement, huh?" He grins. "I have a reputation to protect."

I nod, fighting the urge to drop my towel and put his hands on me.

I might even be willing to beg him.

But I won't. Not today.

Taking the bag from his hands, I give him one last look and say, "Let me change, and then we can go."

"I'll wait in the car," he agrees.

"It's okay," I tell him. "No one else is here."

To work on my physical therapy and workouts for the mild cerebral palsy, Coach lets me use her lunch hour and closes the gym so she and I can work uninterrupted. After I broke my foot several months ago while working out, she insisted on helping me with strength training. It worked. I've never felt stronger or more in control of my body. Now, I love working out and have managed to pull Theo into my yoga routines in the morning. At first he hated it, but after I told him he needed to support my butt when we did a particular pose, he got on board quickly.

Theo nods and takes a seat on the bench in the middle of the lockers.

"All right, I'll wait here."

I take the bag back to the bathrooms to handle the "crime scene," and locate the tampons and a receipt with a phone number written on the back. I crumble the receipt. *Sorry, Nan. Theo will not be calling you anytime soon.*

With a three-pointer Michael Jordan would be proud of, I ring the trash can with Nan's crumpled love note. Sorry, not sorry.

When I'm done in the bathroom, I pull out the clothes Theo thoughtfully brought me. For a moment, with my hands buried in his bag, all I can think is: I'm going to be devastated.

Devastated.

The kind you can never recover from.

I have two more weeks with him.

It won't be enough.

It will never be enough.

Clutched in my hand is a pair of Theo's sweatpants and a Von Bremen T-shirt he wore in high school when he was much smaller. The man brought me his clothes to change into. Soft, comfy clothes. Clothes with his name on the back.

Why? Why did I have to fall in love with him? Why can't I love the Bos of the world? Or even the Thads? Anyone other than a man who has a FastPass to every pussy on campus. A man who wants to travel the world and plow through every fangirl this side of the hemisphere.

Why him?

Because, a little voice whispers in my head, it's fate.

Is it fate?

Or is it bad luck?

Or karma?

Not that I go around acting shitty, but I haven't always been the nicest person. I make mistakes, but I try to atone for them. Hines and Grace raised me that way. And maybe that's why I'm not going with Theo to Washington.

Baseball is our thing, yes, but it's not my life.

When Hines and Grace died, I made a promise I would do something with my life, something that would make them proud. I stand by my promises. And no matter how much I want to stay with Theo, I need to do this.

Madison is my home.

I don't hate it like he does.

I don't wish to travel and see the world. I just want to make a difference. And Madison is a wonderful town to start with.

Shaking off the sadness of losing my best friend, I hurry and change into Theo's clothes, so I don't keep him waiting.

When I'm done, I find him exactly as I left him, head bowed and playing on his phone. His gaze is slow and lazy as he starts at my feet and ends with the messy bun on my head.

His throat works as he tries for a smirk and fails.

"You look like…"

I make a show and give him a little twirl, knowing I look like a drowned cat in his clothes.

"Mine." I stop midtwirl, but he's quick to amend his statement. "I mean my fangirl."

It feels like I've been shot.

Really? He thinks I look like one of those girls who pine over him in his tight baseball pants? I don't think so. I feel my face go squinty.

Fuck his fangirls.

"Are you ready to go?" I ask, trying not to get all bitchy.

He runs a hand through his hair and sighs. "Yeah. You want to ride with me?"

Fuck, no, I don't. Not now. I need some alone time to calm my hormonal ass down.

"Nah. I don't want to leave my car. I'll meet you at home."

I take a deep breath and smile at my roommate. "Thanks for coming to my rescue."

And making me feel treasured, only to take it away and make me feel like no one.

He nods, turning away and heading out the door, leaving me standing with my heart in my hands and his clothes on my back.

I've calmed down and put my crushed heart back where it belongs.

In my hollow chest.

"Do you want bacon?" I call out to a shirtless Theo who is lounging on the sofa, scrolling through the movie options.

"We live in the south," he says with a horrified face. "We always have bacon."

I figured, but you never know. Most days we go healthy. When we don't, we always run it off.

"You don't have to be a smart-ass," I return with a frown.

Okay, so I'm still a little sensitive. Let's blame it on my period.

"Hurry up, McCallister, so I can hug your emotional ass."

His smile is what causes the flutters to tickle my insides.

But rather than let him know how excited I am for him to "hug my emotional ass," I flip him off.

He chuckles, unaffected, and goes back to the TV.

Finally, the food is ready. I load up one plate for us to share and shoo him over so I can sit beside him.

"Mmm...," he groans longingly. "I don't know if I'm going to miss you or these pancakes."

He just has to keep reminding me of our expiration date.

A day when years' worth of friendship will be reduced to keeping in touch on social media.

I don't feel hungry anymore.

Theo, unbeknownst to my change in mood, proceeds to devour most of the food. I just hand it over so he can shovel it in without worrying about spilling syrup on me.

"You don't want any?" he asks with a mouthful of pancakes.

I shake my head. "Did you find anything for us to watch?"

He eyes me curiously and sets the plate down on the coffee table.

I watch him watching me, both of us quiet and dissecting.

Finally, he sighs long and pained before pulling me down on top of him, allowing me to burrow into the crook of his arm. My breath fans across his nipple, and I see chills break out along his chest.

"Are you cold?"

His scolding stare says all it needs to.

Someone else in this house is sensitive.

Ignoring my grin, he snatches the throw blanket off the back of the sofa and covers up his chest, almost smothering me in the process.

I chuckle, perking up tremendously.

But then he turns on a recorded baseball game of our favorite team, and I decide not to be sad that we won't be able to do this much longer and, instead, enjoy today.

I wake with a start.

Giggling is coming from the living room.

I'm not a psycho.

I'm not.

I'm jealous.

I know it's irrational. Trust me, I've been in this situation time and time again.

It never gets any easier.

Never.

Climbing out of the bed, I tell my rational self to fucking chill. Just because Theo spent the afternoon with me, holding me in his arms and dragging those long fingers down my spine does not mean he can't get a quickie in our living room.

I mean, I've seen it before.

Many, many times.

So why am I shucking off my pants, leaving myself in his T-shirt and underwear, as I head out into the open area?

Because I'm a closet asshole.

"Don't mind me." I wave off, covering one side of my face in a show of giving them privacy. "I just need to use the bathroom."

It could be true.

"Oh God, I forgot you had a roommate," the girl of the night adds.

I drop my hand so I can glare at her when I catch Theo's gaze in the lamp light. His cheek twitches as he peels himself off the bottled blonde. He scratches the side of said cheek with his middle finger, and I almost smile.

Almost.

But Barbie interrupts me. "I bet you'll be so happy to get your own place."

My eyes scan for something to throw at her, but I see Theo shake his head.

Whatever. I don't need this kind of negativity in my life.

I forge down the hall and act like she isn't shirtless and stroking my man's leg like she's about to pounce.

No siree.

I march my petty ass straight into our shared bathroom and grab a pair of panties—not the crime scene ones—and a bottle of perfume, and head into Von Bremen's room where I proceed to spritz the ever-loving fuck out of his navy sheets.

And when I think I have them completely saturated, I shove my undies under his pillow for good measure.

Two can play this game, Barbie.

He will be relieved to have his own place, my toned ass.

You have no idea the shit I do for this man.

No. Idea.

Do not think I am his annoying little sister.

Do not think I didn't feel his fingers slipping under the waistband of his sweatpants that were covering my ass.

Do not think I was asleep.

Do not think I didn't feel him lift me and carry me to my room before laying me down and kissing my lips.

Do not think he minds living with me!

Deep breath, Anniston.

Deep fucking breath.

You know he likes to do this.

You know he retreats anytime feelings come into play.

You know this.

Right. I know this.

Barbie is one of a million. Well, not a million. Hopefully, he kept it under twenty-five. The point is, Barbie is no one. She's not a threat to me.

She's a distraction.

I'm the foundation of his thoughts.

Me.

Just me.

I just have to figure out a way to get him to admit it and make a move. We've messed around with this "friends" shit long enough.

Seeing his phone on his dresser, I decide to be extra petty and take it, swiping up and punching in his passcode. STRIKE. So unoriginal, but I doubt he gives a fuck who hacks into his phone. Theo doesn't have a filter. He's relatively an open book.

Except with me.

With me, he likes to keep shit to himself and hum noncommittal answers when I ask him a personal question he doesn't want to answer.

But that's okay though.

I'm good at figuring Von Bremen out.

I close out a few game apps he has running until I get to what I need.

His contact list.

Last time I thinned out the S's and R's. I think tonight I'll take on the T's and hope Barbie's last name is Thomas.

Tucking it into my right hand, so the happy couple on the couch won't see, I hustle back down the hall, the perfume wafting out from behind me.

Fuck.

I didn't put it back in the bathroom.

Oh well. It's too late now. Maybe he won't notice. I leave shit in his room all the time.

"Carry on," I say with an Oscar-worthy fakeness.

I hear Theo chuckle.

"We'll take it to my bedroom," he says with a grin.

I shrug. "Whatever."

Good luck not tasting the amount of perfume I sprayed in there.

I smile sugary sweet. "Goodnight, Teddy."

I don't spare the Barbie on his crotch even a look.

Once I'm back in my room, I make it a point to clean out not only the T's but the M's as well. Even though I can't hear her giggle anymore, I still know she's here. I haven't heard the front door open.

He probably has her mouth busy.

Ugh.

Maybe I'll thin out the P's too.

"I'll call you," I hear from the living room. My door is cracked as usual, and I can see her squeezing him longer than necessary.

Go, girl. Don't look desperate.

"You have my number, right?" Her sexy voice makes me cringe.

"I do."

He did. Hopefully, I deleted it tonight.

If you're disappointed in me, don't be. Theo has 1,825 contacts. Losing five hundred or so is like spitting in the ocean.

He won't notice.

Trust me.

With a long and drawn-out kiss, the woman finally leaves. For a moment, Theo stands at the closed door, his head dropped to his chest. He sighs before flipping the lock and running a hand through his hair and turning and heading toward my door.

Quickly, I push his phone under my pillow and pretend I'm asleep.

I hear the door creak.

"I know you're not asleep," he says in an amused tone.

I'm not ashamed.

I roll over and see him just inside my door, legs crossed, arms folded over his chest.

"Did what's-her-name leave already?"

He smirks, pushing off the wall and coming to sit on the edge of my bed.

"Yeah, she did. Somehow your perfume bottle spilled all over my sheets." His eyebrow arches nearly to his hairline.

I shrug. "Maybe you knocked it over," I offer.

He shakes his head, his finger going to his lips before he slips it into his mouth and bites his nail. "And your underwear?" he accuses, pulling my purple panties out of his pocket and tossing them with the skill of a pitcher in the hamper.

Again, I don't cower. "Must have been from when I did the laundry." I shrug, burrowing down in the covers. "It happens when you have a roommate."

"Uh-huh," he says, standing. "Sure it does." He reaches behind him and grabs the neck of his shirt, leaning over and pulling it over his head. When did he put on a shirt? "Scoot over," he orders, tossing his shirt in my hamper and unbuttoning his jeans.

"What are you doing?" I ask, panicking on what I am going to do with his damn phone.

Both of his eyebrows arch in an "Are you serious?" way. The denim slides down his muscular thighs with such perfection that if he ever threw out his arm, he could easily have a job at a strip club. Women would pay a fortune to have him pop out of a cake or some shit and shake those narrow hips while killing the Happy Birthday song with his horrible singing.

"Well," he drawls, pulling a leg out, "since I can't breathe in my room—" He cuts me an "I know what you did" look. "—I'm sleeping here tonight so it can air out."

I roll my eyes. "I'm sure it's not that bad." I sniff the air. "Okay, maybe it's a little strong."

He laughs, shaking his head as if he doesn't know what to do with me. "I want the right side," he demands, tipping his chin so I move over.

"I don't like the left side," I argue.

"I don't like blue balls. Move over."

He's got a point. I scoot over, taking my pillow—and his phone—with me. Holding open the blankets, he slides in, punches my pillows, and rolls to the side before slipping an arm around me and pulling me to him.

A big, stupid smile adorns my face.

Well, until he says, "Give me my phone so I can set the alarm. I have an early practice tomorrow."

Chapter Eight

Theo

"**I**t's inflamed."

No shit.

"It'll be fine," I argue, ignoring Coach Anderson's stern look. Really. I've had a sore shoulder before. No need in getting dramatic about it just because I can barely move today. What happened to the *"rub some dirt on it and you'll be fine"* approach?

"You need a shot of cortisone and ice."

I disagree with Dr. Phelps's assessment wholeheartedly. I've had a cortisone shot in my elbow before, and it was like liquid fire being shot into my arm. I nearly cried. I'm man enough to admit it. The shit hurt, and I never want another one.

"I'll take the ice and pain reliever."

Coach Anderson lets out a deep, deep sigh. I don't see why he's so frustrated with me saving the team money. Cortisone shots cost a hell of a lot more than ice and pain relievers. I could take both of those at home and save the team even more money. How's that for being a team player? Bet the school never saw that kind of dedication coming when they offered me a scholarship.

"Theo." Coach's voice is tired. "Dr. Phelps's medical opinion is to take down the inflammation immediately. Ice and Tylenol will take time."

I don't see how that's an issue. Time means riding the pine—or bench, whatever you want to call it. What I call it is a fucking vacation.

"I can live with that." I shrug before cringing when the pain zaps through me. I definitely need a pain killer. Pronto.

"You can live with the possibility of your AAA contract being revoked by an injury?"

Goddammit. No, I fucking can't. *Thanks for reminding me of my responsibilities, Coach Anderson.*

No contract with a minor league team means staying here and working for my father in the insurance business. No matter how much I want to stay with Anniston, I won't work for my father. Computers and uncomfortable desk chairs are not for me. Fucking in a desk chair maybe.

But not working.

Don't be a pussy, Theo. Do what you gotta do. Take it like a man.

"Fine, but I need to make a call first."

I'm taking it like a man, but not alone. Judge me if you want, but until you've seen the size of this needle and experienced the medicine within it, you have no idea of the whining I'm about to do. Anniston McCallister is going to have one rough night. She owes me anyway.

Coach hands me my phone because my shoulder had to reiterate the fact it's fucking useless at the moment, and I press the ridiculous icon selfie of Anniston eating a motherfucking Popsicle in my car. She knew it would piss me off when she sent it. But my irritation was quickly extinguished and replaced by pure lust as I analyzed every muscle in her tongue working that yellow Popsicle down to an abnormal shape. The picture had me fifteen minutes late getting to the car. I whacked off more times than I care to admit to that stupid Popsicle picture. Hence the reason it's her contact icon.

She answers on the third ring.

"Do you want healthy or a side of healthy with fat as our main course?"

Dear God, can I keep her?

I smile into the phone.

"I say we go heavy on the carbs *and* high fat content tonight," I supply.

"I couldn't agree more. Okay, I grabbed more Mountain Dew for you. Can you think of anything else you want while I'm at the store?"

Her. Naked. Maybe tied up with a bow?

"Nah. That's all." I hear squeaking from a shitty buggy I'm positive she refused to swap out and cringe before adding, "Hey, do you think you could swing by the clubhouse after you finish?"

That doesn't sound too desperate, does it?

There's a pregnant pause before she says softly, "What's wrong?"

Her voice is shaky, and I feel slightly guilty I cannot, in fact, take this like a man.

I try smiling so she doesn't get the desperation in my tone over the phone. "It's no big deal...," I lie. "Just a little inflammation in my shoulder. Dr. Phelps wants to give me a shot of cortisone—"

She doesn't give me a chance to finish.

"I'm on my way."

Thank God I didn't have to sound like a whiny bitch and tell her I needed a distraction while they did it.

"Thanks, Ans," I mutter, intently aware Coach and Dr. Phelps have gone quiet next to me.

I hear Anniston apologize to someone at the store, but I don't feel bad they have to put back her items. Shit happens. And my girl always puts me first. Deal with it.

We say our goodbyes to each other, and I hang up, already pulling up a social media app. "She'll be here soon, and then you can piss me off for the rest of the night," I say into the treatment room, directing my comment to either of them.

Someone sighs, but I don't look up. One, I'm a teensy bit embarrassed. And two, I don't give a fuck how long they have to stay after work. They knew I was a diva when they offered me the scholarship to pitch for them.

"Be sure to tell security she'll need to be let in," I add at the last minute.

Coach mutters, "I'm sure that wouldn't stop her anyway."

I chuckle. Anniston loves to give Coach Anderson hell, but deep down, they both respect each other.

"It won't, but it'll save him a headache and an incident report later."

Thirty minutes later, security buzzes the treatment room and announces Anniston's arrival. Coach grumbles but labors to the door and lets her in. Anniston McCallister breezes through the threshold smelling all kinds of edible and pins me with a concerned look.

I try to shrug but grimace instead.

"It's not a big deal. I just need to be able to pitch in a few days."

I can tell she wants to argue, but she knows the lengths I will go not to work for my father.

"Don't lie to me, Von Bremen."

"Anniston," Coach soothes, stepping in and putting a hand on her shoulder before we fight in front of them.

I love verbally sparring with McCallister. Someone always ends up heaving and sweating in anger—her—and it does epic things to her tits.

Coach pulls her to the side so Dr. Phelps can fill her in on the condition of my shoulder. Every once in a while, she looks back at me and frowns.

We gotta do what we gotta do, baby, I send her way in the form of a sad smile.

When she's up to date, Dr. Phelps retreats into the medicine room and Anniston and Coach move toward the table where I'm still perched like a hood ornament, a bag of ice strapped to my shoulder.

Here goes my manhood.

Anniston's hand reaches for my hair, and I feel my eyes drift shut with each pull of her fingers. "Are you sure about this?"

What I wouldn't give to skip this and go home...

"No, but I need to pitch," I answer softly, opening my eyes long enough to see her frown.

She nods in understanding, even though I know it pains her to do so. Anniston is very much a believer in conservative medicine. I bet she would have suggested ice and Tylenol too.

"Okay."

Her consent doesn't mean she's happy about it, but regardless, her hands rake through my hair gently, each stroke pulling me closer and closer to her chest. By the time Dr. Phelps returns, bearing a gift of pain, I'm somewhat relaxed.

"All right, Theo, let's get you feeling better."

Technically, a blow job would have me feeling better much faster than this shot, but I don't argue with the good doctor. I doubt he's had an epic blow job in years.

Someone slides the bag off my shoulder, and I suck in a breath. Anticipation is the worst, and Anniston doesn't miss my reaction.

"I'm thinking pizza and porn tonight," she says all innocently. "The pizza will make me feel better and, well, the porn will help you and the unfortunate souls who will reap the aftermath of your next few shitty days. Maybe you'll go easy on them if you aren't so pent up."

A choking sound and an audible gasp can't mask the sound of my laughter. Does my girl know me or what?

"I think you're on to something, McCallister." Except no one will suffer my wrath but you, I want to say. "Maybe porn will put me in a more forgiving mood."

The rest of my comments die off as I feel Dr. Phelps drying my shoulder and promptly cleaning it.

"Try to relax, Theo," he attempts to soothe me.

Not a fucking chance. My body is locked up tight, preparing for the hell that is soon to take place.

"I'm relaxed," I lie.

Anniston makes a noise in her chest like maybe she swallowed wrong or thinks Dr. Phelps is a moron. I know she wouldn't be masking a disbelieving scoff. Now would not be the appropriate time to be a smart-ass.

"Try and relax your shoulders," he tries again. "Lean into Anniston."

Now that's something I *can* do.

Without any further instruction, I bury my face into Anniston's soft tits and almost groan. Almost. I don't want to make it weird, but seriously, her tits are so fucking warm. With a little alcohol, I think I could get away with her letting me motorboat them. But alas, no beer. Or tequila. Tequila really gets her going...

Lost in the daydreams of her pink nipples, I feel Dr. Phelps at my back. Immediately, I'm tense again. It's a fucking big-ass needle. I do not need to explain why I can't relax here.

"You know what I'm looking forward to learning from watching porn tonight?" Anniston's breath feathers against my ear, and chills break out along my arms.

"What?" I whisper back, acutely aware I'm going to be stabbed at any minute.

"I want to…" The warmth of her tongue is what I notice first. Slow and languid, it drifts across my neck, stopping just at my jaw. Instinctively, my hands clench her hips as I try securing her in place. No one needs her darting off when things are just getting interesting.

I swallow. "Don't stop."

For the love of God, don't fucking stop.

With my plea, Anniston's glorious tongue is on the move again. Tempting. Torturous. Until it reaches my lips, and Dr. Phelps jams the fucking needle in my shoulder, and I suck in a harsh breath.

Fuck.

My chest is tight, and all the oxygen feels like it's caught in my throat, but when I finally manage out a groan, Anniston's lips descend on mine and the pain doesn't seem as excruciating anymore.

She's kissing me.

Anniston McCallister is kissing me.

Sure, we've kissed before, but not like this.

Not opened mouthed with my hands inching up her ribs, my thumb daring to slide beneath the underwire of her bra.

Keep going on my shoulder, Doc. Whatever you do, don't let this moment end.

I have a feeling it won't happen again.

"Almost done, Theo. You're doing great."

I barely register his praise. All I can think is: Anniston McCallister is the best fucking kiss I've ever had. Her tongue moves in tandem with mine. Fighting. Clashing. But yielding when she recognizes I run the oral game. She wins the distraction, but I own this goddamned kiss.

Every move is small and dainty, and my God, do I want to rough her up. I want to demand she show me how she licked that Popsicle in my vintage '67 Mustang.

But I don't.

"All done," Coach announces with a little more happiness than I feel is warranted for breaking up mine and Anniston's cuddle time.

Anniston pulls away and wipes her mouth. Her face is flushed when she says, "See? That wasn't so bad, was it?"

I could break the tension with a shitty lie about the kiss being like kissing my sister, but I don't want to. She expects me to lash out because that's what I do. I'm rude and shy away from emotions, especially when it comes to her.

But I can't do it.

The kiss wasn't bad.

It wasn't like kissing my sister.

It was patient.

It was full of unspoken words.

The kiss, even if it was meant to be a distraction, was epic.

It should be memorialized, not tarnished or branded with a lie.

So instead of being a dick, I go with a subject change instead.

"We can get that stupid stuffed crust pizza garbage you like." I try to shrug, but Dr. Phelps is wrapping my shoulder, and I end up making a face of pain.

The fake smile Anniston flashes me feels foreign. I don't get her fake smiles. I get real ones. Always.

"Okay. I guess we can get your stupid meat lovers' toppings, even though I'd rather have ham and pineapple."

The kiss wasn't *that* good. I'm not eating fruit on my pizza.

"Stuffed crust meat lovers it is," I confirm, looking back to see if Dr. Phelps is almost fucking done. Things are getting awkward in here, and I'm ready to go. Anniston and I need normalcy. "Can we go?" I ask Coach.

He leans behind me to look at Dr. Phelps's progress.

"Yeah, you can go. Take it easy for the next few days. All right?"

I nod my consent. At this point, I would agree to anything to get out of here.

Anniston grabs my phone, and I ease off the table.

"I assume you're riding home with me," she says, unlocking my phone and doing who knows what to my contacts. I know she deletes names. I know my once two thousand contacts did not disappear when I upgraded my phone. I let her keep her form of retaliation.

I scare off her dates, and she deletes mine.

We're petty like that.

We're in love like that.

"Why would I ride with you?" I ask absently. Where the fuck is my bag? Did I bring it in here or leave it by my locker?

"Uh," she says all smug, "because you have only one functioning arm at the moment."

No.

"I'm not leaving my car here."

Seriously, I don't have many friends here. People speak to me, but we're not friends. There is no way I am leaving my car out here to be keyed or worse.

Anniston sighs and looks at Coach.

"He can't help you," I argue. "I'm not leaving my fucking car, Anniston."

She rolls her eyes before finally turning the phone around.

"Thad will get someone to drop him off. He can stay with us tonight."

"No."

She arches a brow, and I almost growl.

"Fine. But pizza and porn night are still on." I arch my brow, mimicking hers, then add. "You're sleeping with me. Thad can take your room."

Chapter Nine

Anniston

The apartment is quiet when I finish with my shower. A quick look around the corner reveals an exhausted Theo asleep on the sofa. Thad is relaxed in the chair watching TV on mute.

"You can turn it up," I tell Thad, nodding in Theo's direction. "The noise won't wake him." Not when he's this tired.

"It's fine. I'm not really watching it anyway."

I shrug, drying my hair with Theo's oversized towel. I couldn't use my towel; it's wrapped around my body. "Do you want anything from the kitchen?"

It's the least I can do since he brought pizza and Theo's car home.

"I'm good, thank you," he says politely. His momma would be proud of the man he's become.

I nod, realizing he's not up for talking, and slip inside my bedroom to change. I go with my own pajamas tonight, a sleep shirt and knee-high socks. Yes, it looks ridiculous, but it's comfy. And when you're tired, nothing beats comfort.

When I've managed to brush through the tangles and pull my hair into something resembling a beehive, I pad into the living room and see Theo has awakened. His clothes are rumpled, and his face is marred with a frown.

"Are you okay," I ask, coming around to sit alongside him.

"Why are you wearing that?"

Why does he sound so pissed off? I look down at the shirt I've worn a dozen times.

"What do you mean? I always wear this."

He scrubs a hand over his face and glares when Thad laughs.

"We have a guest," he grits out.

"Duh," I respond maturely. "Thad has seen me in this before."

Thad coughs awkwardly, and Theo's face turns red.

I look between the two brothers.

"What? At least I have underwear on. I usual—"

"For fuck's sake, Ans. Just stop."

What is Theo's deal? He just spooned me for eight solid hours last night. I had less on last night than I do today.

Attempting to change the subject, I go with, "How's your shoulder?"

He takes a deep breath, and his voice loses the hard edge it had earlier. "Stiff but better."

I smile, fussing with the blanket on his lap. "Do you want me to get you anything?"

He shakes his head and then looks at his brother. "No. Just the porn you promised me."

Thad groans and stands. "I'm off to bed. I'll see you two in the morning."

Theo waves him off.

"Goodnight," I add. "Thank you for all the help tonight."

Thad flashes me a genuine smile before staring at Theo with a look I can't decipher.

When the door to my bedroom closes, Theo finally turns back to me.

"Are we going with my collection or yours?"

I scoff. "What? I don't have porn."

The twitch of his mouth says he's joking. "I've seen under your bed, McCallister," he drawls. "Terrible hiding spot by the way."

This man.

"They're yours! You put them there the last time your parents came for a visit."

He grins. "You don't need to lie, Ans. I'm not judgy."

He's a damn fool, but I can't help but laugh.

"Fine," I relent, letting him keep his teasing. "We'll go with yours since the ones under my bed are clopping porn."

I shake my head like I'm ashamed, and he laughs, pushing at my shoulder with his good arm. "They are not."

They aren't furry porn based on cartoon characters, but I probably wouldn't care if they were. That's how hard up I am for this man.

"You ready now or want to eat something?" I change the subject.

He didn't eat much tonight. Not that I monitor him like a baby, but when you live with a guy who's also an athlete, you get used to huge portions of food. So when he only eats one piece of pizza instead of four or five, you worry he may be sick.

"I'm fine." He waves off my concern and kicks off the blankets I piled on top of him when he fell asleep. "Come on," he orders, struggling to his feet. I don't offer to help him because sometimes when he's hurt, he isn't in the best of moods. I'm not looking to get my feelings hurt and sleeping on the sofa, so I don't have to sleep next to him.

I busy myself with putting the food up and turning off all the lights when Theo finally lies down in the bed, his TV lighting up the hallway.

I feel awkward tonight, and I'm not sure why. Last night we slept together. Hell, I can't count the number of times we've slept in the same bed. We've even watched porn together. Well, not really. I've caught him watching porn, and I might have hidden like a stalker and watched him longer than I intended.

But never have we watched porn in the bed. Together. Under the covers.

I shouldn't be nervous. If I told Theo I didn't want to watch porn in the bed with him, he would turn it off and never say anything about it. But I feel like this is a test. He knows I sabotage his dates and delete contacts out of his phone.

He knows.

And this is his test.

Are we friends or not?

I vote not, but what if I totally mess this up? I've never had a boyfriend longer than a day or two. I don't know if I know what to do with a man or even how to keep one.

"Anniston!" comes a loud voice that will probably get us a text from the neighbors to keep it down.

"I'm coming!" I holler back softer than him, but still loud enough to get a complaint.

Under the covers, reclined on a mound of pillows, lies the man I'd do anything for.

"I figured you'd want to watch the one with the pizza delivery guy and the hot college student." He tries to shrug but forgets his shoulder is taped up, so he settles for an eye roll.

"What if I wanted the one where the baseball player boned the batgirl?" I return with a smile, sliding under the covers and purposely trying to avoid touching him.

90

"Hmm…," he muses. "I'm not sure I have that one… Unless you want to dip into my private stash?"

I half laugh. One, the stupid videos those girls filmed on his phone have long been deleted. He would know if he ever watched them. And two, Theo doesn't bang the batgirls. He likes the ones who know nothing about the sport other than they run and throw a baseball.

Please… a batgirl.

"I think dipping into your private stash would end up with us praying for your soul tonight."

All a lie.

He may frequent bedrooms, but he's a giving lover, or so I've heard. He's also very upfront with what he's looking for. Basically, a wet hole. He doesn't care which.

"You may be right," he adds quietly, the air in the room changing into something more serious.

I glance over to see what his deal is. His eyes are focused intently on the blue screen while his hand clenches the remote.

"Are you okay?"

I lay my hand over his and he flinches.

Okay. Don't touch him.

Sighing, he turns off the TV and scoots down into the blankets. "Would you mind if we just went to bed? I'm more tired than I thought."

What happened?

Were we not just playing around?

Swallowing thickly, I nod and offer him a sad smile. "Sure. I'll just put in my headphones and listen to music."

With a curt nod, he rolls over and turns off the light on his side, never turning back to face me.

Okay then.

Finding Theo's headphones on the bedside table, I plug them into my phone and turn out the light, plunging us into darkness.

Sleep normally comes easily to me but not tonight. Tonight, my mind races and I worry if I said something wrong. Is Theo mad at me? Does his shoulder hurt?

I'm confused and probably more emotional than I should be about him shutting down and not snuggling with me like he usually does.

I'm scrolling through my phone while Dermot Kennedy's soulful voice fills my ears when I come across a video that plays over the music.

"You're ridiculous," says the girl in the beautiful ball gown, twirling barefoot in the grass.

It's a video of me and Theo on prom night. No one had asked me to prom, and I almost didn't go when Theo said we could go together.

"It's not ridiculous. Come dance with me. It's the last time it's acceptable for you to step on my feet and get away with it."

In the video, I stop twirling, my hair already falling down out of the intricate updo that took Grace an hour to do.

Theo zooms in on my face, recording the want in my eyes. I remember I wanted to dance with him more than anything. But after he was pulled away by girl after girl, I gave up, wandering out to the baseball field where I didn't have to hear the swoons and breathy promises of a great after-party at hotel rooms they had secured.

I wasn't that mad.

I was used to Theo being center of attention.

I was used to being his sidekick.

I was used to coming second in his life.

But then he came, his bow tie unknotted, his hair disheveled, and a frown on his face. He had asked what I was doing on the field. I remember telling him I liked the way the grass felt between my toes.

He didn't laugh.

Instead, he took off his own shoes and asked me to dance.

My voice in the video interrupts the memory.

"Okay," I say hesitantly.

The camera switches to selfie-mode and Theo's dimple fills the screen. He's smiling, taking my hand, and twirling me around before handing me the camera. I fumble, but I find a hold with my hands around his neck and his around my waist.

"Say you're gonna miss me, McCallister," he says softly.

I remember panicking, wondering what the right thing to say was. Funny. Nothing has changed four years later. I'm still the same girl who wants more from him but is too scared to say it. Too scared to lose the only person I have left. The only person who's looked out for me. In high school the fear came from rejection. Now, as an adult, the fear is being alone. Without someone to have dinner with. To watch games with. I wish someone would have sent me to charm school where I could have learned to be more social with girls.

I could have had more friends and then losing Theo wouldn't be so detrimental.

But that wasn't the case.

I stuffed every memory and every dream in his pocket. I kept him close. I loved him in secret, and in a couple weeks, I'll have nothing. All of it will be a distant memory.

"I might miss you a little," teases the younger girl in the video.

She's lying. She's going to miss him a whole hell of a lot. But back then he meant when he went away to college, before we knew we would end up living together.

"I'm gonna miss you a little too," he returns softly.

Gah, we were so stupid back then.

Okay, fine. We're still stupid. We've made no headway whatso-ever since then.

I stare at the screen, watching the girl smile and twirl in the arms of the boy she dreamt of marrying. As their bodies sway, the crickets chirping in the background, I find my hand inching down my sleep shirt until I reach the hem. Carefully, I slip it up my hips, so as not to wake Theo sleeping next to me.

Theo's laugh in the video makes me smile, and my hand works underneath my panties. Chills break out over my stomach, and I close my eyes, listening to his eighteen-year-old voice on the video.

"I won't bite, McCallister. You can come closer."

The pads of my fingers find the sensitive nub at my center and apply pressure, causing a groan to slip from my lips.

"I am close," I argue on camera, the audio of the video playing the background noise to my fantasy. Delicately, I massage the bundle of nerves until my panties are damp against my skin. Shivers take over as my skin turns from chilled to blazing hot.

"Oh, God," I murmur, biting the sheet at my chin, my back arching as my knees bend, allowing my hand better access.

"Not close enough," he says, and I nearly come from his statement alone. Faster, my fingers work, dipping lower and smearing the wetness around. I'm lost in his voice when suddenly the video stops playing.

What the hel—

I can't see shit, but what I can see has me swallowing harshly. A hand—not mine—hovers over the pause button.

Fuck.

He can sleep through an earthquake and this wakes him? You have got to be shitting me.

Theo pulls the earbuds from my ears, and I let him.

I'm not about to do it myself and let him see where my hand was. Although, he probably already knows, but let me have this hope.

Clearing his throat, his unplugs the headphones and tosses them on the floor.

"You know," he starts, scooting closer and slipping his hand under the covers, placing it on my stomach, "I waited all night to dance with you." He makes a noise low in his throat. "I looked everywhere for you." His hand creeps down to my thigh. "And there you were, dressed like a royal princess, playing in the damn dirt."

I go to argue that I was in the grass and not in the dirt, but his hand covers the hand currently still in my panties. He doesn't make a move to slip under them. He just leaves it there. Resting. Flinching.

"I knew then, I was never going to be able to let you go."

Oh God. Can you come from just words alone? I think I'm about to give it a shot.

"Press play," he whispers by my ear. When I hesitate, he adds, "Unless you're scared."

He was never going to let me go.

I'm never going to let him go either.

I press the play button, and his voice sounds over the speakers this time.

"Now you're close," he praises on camera.

Chapter Ten

Theo

I couldn't have timed it better. I don't know what exactly woke me, but I'd like to think my body has an internal alarm when Anniston McCallister is being naughty.

"Now you're close," says my younger self when things were much simpler between me and Anniston. Before her grandparents died and set our relationship back. I couldn't very well ask her out when she was grieving. And then when we moved in together, things just got even more fucked up.

I was pent up. She was grieving, working hard to make her grandparents proud. She didn't need me to barge into her plans and derail her. She needed a constant. She needed a friend. And I thought that's all we'd ever be.

Until I woke up to her moans.

Until I woke up to her pleasuring herself to our prom video.

It's a sign.

She could have been getting off to anything. *Magic Mike. Fifty Shades of Grey*. But she wasn't. She was turned on by us dancing. And if that doesn't make me rock-fucking-hard, then I don't know what else will.

"Keep going," I tell her, my voice husky.

I hear her gulp, and it makes me grin. Tortuously, I pull my hand from atop hers and pull her leg over mine, opening her fully. Her panties are still on, and as much as I would like to rip them clear off her body, I don't. If I lose that barrier between us, there is no telling the mistakes I will make tonight.

"Don't get scared now, McCallister," I taunt, appealing to the competitive side of her. "Be brave."

Be my fucking fantasy.

My hand drifts along her thigh, across the lace of her panties until it's resting on top of hers again. The dampness there is almost my breaking point. If my shoulder wasn't taped up, I'd probably jerk off alongside her.

But alas, karma is a petty bitch.

"Lower," I tell her, taking control of this situation.

A small sound, almost a whimper, seeps from her lips as I push her hand lower, lining it up for what I want to do next.

"Now slide one finger in."

Her leg quivers against me, and I pin it close to my body.

"Do it," I encourage.

Anniston expels a breath, and I feel her body relax as if she's accepted the fact she isn't getting out of this. Her back arches, and the moan she lets out has my dick jumping at my pants, attempting to get free and help her.

Down, boy, not this time.

This time? What the fuck am I talking about? This can't happen again. I'm leaving soon.

Her breathy voice interrupts my internal struggle.

"What now?"

Ugh! What now? Now, I want you to sit on my fucking face until you come down my fucking cheek.

With my palm, I add pressure to her hand, forcing it deeper inside her. "Add another finger," I say when she gasps from the intrusion.

My hand twitches as it's everything I can do to keep it from diving inside her panties.

"Spread them apart, stretch yourself..."

She does as I ask, her stomach sinking in and out with her heavy breaths. I have to end this before I come in my fucking pants. Pushing her hand down and out of my way, I tell her to keep fingering herself, and then I make the most fatal mistake of my life and put the pad of my finger to her clit and rub until she calls out my name.

If I buy chocolate and dinner it will be like PMS week. Anniston won't think it's a big deal, right? Or even if we went out for Mexican food later... Neither of these ideas scream *I love you*, right? We're friends and roommates. It would be awkward if we didn't do something for her birthday.

She's single.

I'm single.

We have no prior commitments for tonight.

Granted, I could go out and get laid for my time and dinner, but I'm not in the mood. I'd rather swing by the grocery store, grab a pint of ice cream and some tacos from the food truck across from the campus, and watch game footage with Ans.

That's what friends do.

Chill.

We would be chilling together on her birthday. Together. But not together.

Oh, for fuck's sake. Why do I give a shit? I'm gonna stop for food. She can eat or not. And if she wants some of my ice cream, I might share it with her.

After the night that will forever go down as one of the best nights of my life, Anniston and I have been different toward each other. Not necessarily awkward, more like hesitant. Each joke is weighed in our heads before we say it, which is never what we've done before. Both of us have zero verbal filters, so actually thinking before we speak to each other has made it a little quiet around here, to say the least.

Passing each other in the hall in a towel is a whole different kind of issue.

My dick has laid claim to that body, and it's all I can do to prevent him from convincing me to grab that clingy-ass towel and toss it out the window where it can never cover her body again. Not to mention the lack of restraint on her part. My contact list is now down to fifty-five names. All of them are guys, except for my mom and our dry cleaner. I've even found two pairs of her underwear in my gym bag. Anniston McCallister is staking her claim.

Things are definitely complicated.

The problem is, she's still not willing to go to Washington, and I'm still not ready to settle down. We're a fucking disaster.

After I spend nearly a half hour debating on what to do for Anniston's birthday, I step out of the car and drag my tired ass into the locker room. Despite tracking Anniston's phone—it's for her own protection, not because I've become obsessed—and seeing she's still at the library studying, I have no motivation to practice. The only practicing I want to do is with her. Practicing with the team is a formality anyway. I don't learn anything from it other than how to be a team player. Kind of.

It's a waste of time.

Time that I could use for writing down the pros and cons of taking Anniston out to dinner or staying in where no one can steal any glances of her.

That's it. I should skip practice. I'm due for a stomachache or some tendinitis.

"Von Bremen!"

Also, I wouldn't have to deal with the smell of armpits and ball sweat after being surrounded with Anniston's body lotion that I'm sure was developed by Salem witches. I was out... It happens. The shit makes my dick twitch every time I get a whiff. I can't even narrow down the exact scent that makes me crazy. But I can tell you it makes me think of sunscreen, which then makes me think of her in a bikini. And visions of her in a bikini take me on this path of envisioning her tits underneath said bikini, which all leads to me jerking off until I come all over that fucking lotion bottle.

Voodoo magic.

There's no other explanation for it.

And yes, I rinse it off for her. Jeez. I'm not inconsiderate.

"Dude."

Someone knocks into me from behind.

"What's up your ass?"

I could *not* turn around.

I could grab my stomach and heave. No one would be the wiser. No one would know I was faking sick. Especially not Toby.

"McCallister is up his ass... Fucking up all those pretty little thoughts of his."

Ugh. But Brody would know. You don't have a catcher you've been friends with all four years of college and he not pick up on your lies. And since he's already talking shit today, I know I won't be able to blow off this practice without him causing a scene. Who gives a fuck that he's sort of correct about Anniston fucking up my thoughts?

With a deep, exaggerated sigh, I toss my phone in my locker and slowly turn around, raising my middle finger so it presses directly into Brody's chest.

"Aww, don't be mean, Von Bremen. I can't help it if McCallister leaves you with blue balls every day."

I could punch Brody in the face to get out of this practice. Not only is it unsportsmanlike conduct, but it will bruise my pitching hand. Problem solved.

My gaze drags up Brody's increasing gut, and I make a face. "At least I'm not eating my feelings, dick."

Brody, never one to take my shit, barks out a hearty laugh and shoves me into Toby, who quickly rights us both.

Shame.

Falling could have sent me home too.

"Come on, man, what's your deal? I can't have you throwing like shit out on the field and running extra laps."

I cut him a look. I've *never* thrown like shit. Ever. Not since Anniston's grandfather helped me hone my craft. And definitely not since Anniston took his place and runs my training schedule like a major league pitching coach.

Shit is never a term associated with my pitching.

I sigh, taking a seat on the bench. With my head in my hands, I admit to the floor, "It's Anniston's birthday today, and I'm not sure what to do."

Brody howls like a woodland animal. "The playboy has been played," he crows. "Tell me, Von Bremen, does she have you by the balls with one hand or two?"

Who needs friends really? They are such a pain in the ass.

I spit on Brody's bare feet under me, and I feel pleasantly vindictive when he jumps back and hushes that atrocious howling.

Toby chuckles under his breath at our exchange and says, "What did you have in mind for her?"

See, Toby, I don't fucking know because the last time we really had a quiet night together, I nearly came in my sheets that smelled like her goddamned perfume.

I groan. "I don't know. It's the last birthday I'll get to spend with her for a while."

"Well, well, he has a heart after all," chimes in Brody who apparently found a paper towel and cleaned his foot.

"Don't be a dick." Seriously, I've had a bad couple of days. "You know her birthday is a big deal to her."

When Brody's smug smile turns into something solemn, I imagine him remembering Anniston's birthday is also the day her mom died. She doesn't shy away from celebrating her birthday, but she never bothers with a party.

My stomach cramps thinking of me being across the country playing a game and not being able to celebrate with her. What if she doesn't celebrate? What if she does? What if she celebrates with Thad?

Oh God.

"Look, dude," says Brody, clasping me on the shoulder, "why don't you bring her over to the house, grab a cake, and we'll play some poker. She likes that, right?"

She does, but I kind of wanted to celebrate it with just the two of us.

I think of the sounds she made as she came underneath my hand. Maybe Brody is right. Maybe I shouldn't keep her all to myself. Dangerous things could happen to us. Things we can never erase or move on from.

I've waited this long.

There's no need to ruin what we have before I leave.

Anniston needs a man who will put her first, and as much as I want to believe that man is me, it's not. If it was, I would break my contract and work for my father. But I can't. I just fucking can't.

And for that reason alone, I agree.

"Yeah, sounds good. I'll text her."

After practice, a sense of dread settles in the pit of my stomach.

I *really* don't want to go over to Brody's tonight, but I also don't want to make these last few days any more awkward than they already are. If this was last year, we would have gone to a party. We always go to parties. Anniston likes hanging out with the guys and talking shit. This shouldn't be so depressing for me.

This is what we do for fuck's sake.

"You're home early," she calls from the front door. "Did they let you out of practice early?"

Coach Anderson knew I was full of shit when I claimed I had a stomachache, but he still let me go.

"Yeah, the coach said I was so good that I just took up space in the dugout." I chug the water in my hand and swallow. "He also said they needed to work with the losers more so there was no need in me staying on account of their suckiness."

I shrug and fight a grin, looking at the faint smile on her face.

"What did you do?"

My eyebrows arch in shock. "I'm serious. I can't help it if everyone else sucks."

Finally, she breaks her composure and laughs.

There it is.

My fucking happy place.

Exactly the way I like to end my days.

Her lithe body moves into the kitchen and playfully shoves me away from the refrigerator.

"What do you want to eat tonight?"

You.

"I was thinking we could go to this party over at the team's house and then finish the night off at Mae's."

At exactly 10:02 p.m. when she made her entrance into the world.

I shrug at her confused expression. "Since it's your birthday and all."

Her face falls slightly.

Does she look disappointed?

Fuck. I never should have listened to Brody. He hasn't had a girlfriend since he switched to tighty-whities.

"I mean, if you want to," I amend quickly.

It takes her a minute, but she finally smiles and confirms, "Yeah, sounds fun."

Fun.

Yeah, it's going to be a fucking blast.

Chapter Eleven

Anniston

I tried not to seem disappointed when I texted a friend, giving away the two tickets for the Braves game I bought earlier for my birthday. I figured it was the last time Theo and I would be able to attend a game together for a long time.

He made other plans.

And that's fine. It really is.

Okay, so I'm disappointed, but as long as we spend my birthday together, then it doesn't matter.

"Ans, are you almost ready?"

I give myself one last glance in the mirror. My hair is down for once, styled in trendy beach waves. My shorts are probably too short, but it's hot as fuck, so I really don't care. At least they are high-waisted and shave an inch or so off my waistline, so the long-sleeve crop top is extra flattering.

"Anniston!" he shouts again. Impatient much?

"I'm coming," I mutter, grabbing my wristlet off the dresser and throwing open the door, nearly colliding with Theo.

"I said I was coming," I tell him with a frown.

"You never take that long to get ready," he accuses like he suspects I was back here building a bomb or something. His eyes rake up and down my body leisurely before he swallows thickly. "You look beautiful." His voice is sincere and reverent, and it makes me want to come clean.

I don't want to go to this party. I want to stay here with him and celebrate alone. After the night when we took our loose boundaries to a whole other level, I've been even more anxious about him leaving.

I won't admit it to him, but I started looking into colleges in Washington. I know you aren't supposed to follow a man, but Theo isn't just any man. He's my man. He has been for years, and if I stay here, I'm going to lose him.

I tuck a strand of hair behind my ear and smile. "Thanks, Teddy. You don't look so bad yourself."

It's not a lie. His jeans sit low on his hips, and he's thrown on a stupid T-shirt that Brody bought him one year for Christmas. It says, "The king of the backdoor slider." I laughed at first since a backdoor slider is a type of pitch. One that Theo throws very well, but it's also a metaphor he and his teammates use for anal. Then I realized how very true that shirt is, in more ways than one.

I wanted to burn it.

I didn't, clearly.

I can keep my crazy in check… sometimes.

"You want to take my car?" he asks hesitantly, like we're on a date.

No. I'd like to stay here. With you. Naked. In the shower.

"Sure, that'd be great."

Liar. I am such a fucking liar.

The party is in full swing by the time we arrive. In a matter of ten minutes, Theo has already chugged a beer. He's working on beer number two while sitting across from me at the poker table.

I thought maybe his bad mood was because he felt awkward giving me a gift earlier. When we parked on the curb and unbuckled our seat belts, he pulled out a half-ass wrapped gift from the back seat, thrusting it in my hands.

"You can't open it until your actual birthday," he said, looking at his watch and informing me, "at 10:02 p.m. to be exact."

I laughed, thinking he was joking.

He didn't.

It was a little awkward, so I nodded and tucked it away, promising to wait.

Theo isn't great at buying gifts, but he always manages to do something. Even if it's just chocolate or toilet paper. I didn't think it was a big deal.

Apparently, I was wrong.

"Your turn, Von Bremen," Brody observes, kicking at Theo's chair when all he does his stare down at the table with a definitive frown.

Something is going on with him, but I don't know what. Did he have plans and my birthday got in the way? Surely not. Theo has always spent my birthday with me.

"I fold," he says dryly, tossing his cards on the table.

"What the fuck, man?" Brody is done with his shit already. "We just fucking started. Why did you tell us to deal you in?"

Theo's gaze finds mine.

Because I wanted to be dealt in, and he wasn't leaving me alone with a table full of his teammates.

What the fuck are we doing?

Why are we even here if he's going to act like an asshole? This isn't the birthday party I wanted.

This was *his* idea!

"I had a shitty hand," he lies, eyeing the guy next to me. I think his name is Rhys. He's a junior, second string utility player, which basically means he can play multiple positions. Utility players are in high demand in the major leagues. Not so much for second stringers though. Although, with Rhys's all-American good looks, he would be great marketing for a potential team.

I roll my eyes at Theo's behavior before he gets up, claiming he needs to get another beer.

Great.

That's exactly what we need—a pissed off *and* drunk Theo. Tonight is shaping up well. Hello future birthdays, let's plan a quiet night in front of the TV or at the gym. Either will work. Either is my happy place.

"Let's play blackjack since Theo is bipolar. At least the games are shorter for when he needs to change his tampon."

I glance over at a smiling Rhys. He nods my way as if he just did me a solid. Part of me wants to shove him to the floor for the simple fact he is talking shit about my man. The other part of me takes offense he might think I can't play poker without Theo.

Who do you think taught Theo?

Dudes, I swear. When will they ever learn women are better at most things than they are? It's science.

Brody interrupts my plotting by grunting out something unintelligible. He won't stand for Rhys talking about his friend either.

Theo hasn't returned when Brody deals, and I briefly wonder if I should go look for him but then decide he might need a minute to settle down.

"So, Anniston," Rhys starts, licking his lips like a total predator, "what are you going to do when Von Bremen takes off?" He nods to the kitchen where Theo wandered off to. "You're staying here, right? Going to medical school?"

Is there a billboard somewhere with a countdown until Von Bremen leaves?

I narrow my eyes at the man who I would have totally gone for had Von Bremen never wandered into my life. Although, I may need to adjust my standards after he leaves.

"Umm, I'm moving back home to Madison, my hometown," I admit with a baby shrug. It's Theo's hometown too. I'll be stranded alone in a town where the memories will be thick and rich with our history.

Rhys nods. "What kind of doctor do you want to be?"

Please, Rhys, spare us both from the terrible small talk. Holding back a cringe, I smile instead and answer him like Grace would have wanted. "Sports medicine."

A career working with the athletes of the sports I love so much.

"That's cool."

Yeah, real cool, Rhys.

Standing, I try not to look uninterested at anything he has to say. "If you'll excuse me, I need to check on Theo."

Brody is quick to answer me, his eyes darting to the kitchen. "He's fine. Just getting another drink. Sit. Let's play."

Uh, let's not and track the sounds of laughter coming from the kitchen until we find the source.

It's a girl I haven't seen before.

"Vanessa is Seth's sister," Brody supplies.

I don't care if she's Mother Theresa's sister. The way her hands are rubbing down his chest have me enraged.

Calm down, Anniston. Calm your crazy ass down.

You're friends.

So what if he helped you come so hard you saw stars? So what if you love him?

So what if he's leaving? He never made you any promises. You were the one reading too much into this.

This is what happens when you think you found your soul mate at fourteen.

Disappointment.

A warm hand lands on my arm as I watch Theo standing there, hands in his pockets, while Vanessa gets close enough she could slobber on *my* damn dimple.

I hope her breath smells like butthole.

"Want to get out of here?"

I whip around and stare at the tan hand on my skin. I stare at that hand like it holds all the answers in the world.

Maybe it does.

Maybe it's the shove I need.

Theo and I are friends.

Just. Fucking. Friends.

It was stupid to attempt to build anything with Theo when he's about to leave.

Slowly, I raise my face and stare at Rhys's green eyes. He's cute. He's chatty. At least I won't spend my birthday alone.

"Yeah." I sigh. "I want to get out of here."

"Anniston—"Brody starts, attempting to calm the situation.

But I'm done. So freaking done.

"Thanks for having me over, Brody. I'll see ya around."

Ignoring his pleas to stay, I let Rhys pull me out the front door to his Jeep parked on the curb.

"Rhys! If you take one more goddamned step, I will break your fucking leg."

My head falls forward at the sound of his voice. I feel like I have whiplash. This back and forth is exhausting.

"I'll make sure she gets home, Von Bremen. Enjoy the party favors."

Bad move, Rhys.

Theo bounds down the steps—where did he get a bat—and eats up the space between us. His eyes are hard and unforgiving.

"Get in the fucking car. We're going home."

Say what?

"Rhys can take me home. You've been drinking."

And you pissed me off.

"Anniston, no one has time for your pettiness. Get in the god-damned car!"

My heart. It just stopped.

Am I being petty by leaving? Am I being petty because I feel betrayed by my best friend on my birthday?

Is he being petty by not allowing me to save face and leave with Rhys?

I guess it doesn't matter. Tonight has just gone to shit.

I clear the knot blocking my airway and hold my head up high and meet Theo's angry glare, his jaw clenching with barely contained rage.

"I don't want to go home with you, Theo."

He reels back like I hit him. His head cocks to the side and grins like something feral.

And then I cry.

I tried to hold it in but nothing, not even pinching my hand, makes it stop.

"Let me go, Theo. Let me leave with Rhys."

A harsh breath whooshes out as the shock of what I said sinks in.

I can't believe I said it myself.

Rhys has been quiet up until now, and the idiot he is decides now is the best time to step in. "I'll get her home safe, Theo."

That shocks him out of it, and he slips back behind his trademark asshole.

"You know what you can do, Rhys? You can take your subpar ass back in the house and spit bullshit lines at the rest of the gullible girls in there. This one—" He looks at me, his mouth tight at the corners. "—is mine."

If I didn't just feel like I was put through a meat grinder, I would be able to appreciate that he said I was his. Instead, I choose the fact he thinks I'm gullible and can't function without him.

When did I become that girl? When did my whole life revolve around one person?

I hear steps behind me, and then as Rhys passes, he murmurs out a hateful, "Asshole." When Rhys is inside the house, Theo's shoulders slump and he drops the bat to the ground. "Ans," he whispers, but it's too late.

It's far too late for an apology.

"I just want to go home."

He sighs, raking his hands through his hair, and nods, digging his keys out of his pocket.

"I'm driving," I tell him. He's had far too many. I don't give a shit how much he loves his car; he isn't driving drunk.

"Okay," he concedes quietly, passing me the keys. We walk in silence to the car, and when I crank it up, we ride in that same silence until I'm parked, up the stairs, and at my bedroom door.

"I—" he starts.

"Do not say you're sorry," I clip. "We both know you would be lying."

He nods.

I knew he wasn't sorry.

"Goodnight, Theo."

I push open my door, and his tortured voice stops me. "Wait," he pleads.

I am so done with this day. So. Damn. Done.

"What, Theo? What is so damn important that it can't wait until morning?"

He swallows, his throat working hard before looking at his watch. "It's 10:02."

Motherfucker.

Do not do this. Do not make me love you anymore than I already do.

He shoves into my hand the same package he gave me in the car.

"Just know, you'll always be my girl."

I can't deal with this.

"Happy Birthday, Anniston."

The fucking tears are back, dripping all over the terrible wrapping he did with the school's newspaper.

I try sucking it up, but when I fail, I leave it at, "Goodnight, Teddy."

Chapter Twelve

Theo

The next morning, I feel like shit. A big, steamy pile of shit. And Thad has been happy to remind me of it with a steady stream of texts.

Thad: What did you do?!

Thad: She's not answering!

Thad: Brody said you acted like an asshole. Theo, talk to me!

Thad: I can't believe you. It was her birthday!

Thad: You don't deserve her.

He's right. I don't deserve her. Especially after what I let happen last night. But that's the thing, I never deserved her. Ever. And yet, she loves me anyway. I know she does. But I'm trying to do the right thing. I'm trying to set her free, even if I don't want to.

I hated spending her birthday at the team's house. I hated sharing her with all those other guys. So I tried drinking it away. And when Rhys kept staring at her tits, I had to get up or I was going to level his jaw with Brody's baseball bat.

And then fucking Vanessa had to join the festivities.

I can't even remember what she said. All I could do is glare at Brody and Rhys, who were seconds away from having to jerk off in the bathroom because Anniston smelled that fucking good.

And… she wore *the* shorts.

Any time she wears the cutoffs, she gets attention.

Every. Single. Time.

They are her lucky charm.

The ace in the hole.

Her precious.

And she wore them last night in the midst of my horny team-mates. I couldn't deal. I could not fucking deal. At all.

So I entertained Vanessa's ramblings. I let her invade my personal space and make Anniston jealous like she was making me. I'm supposed to let her go, and I can't.

I tried.

I tried acting like we're only friends. I tried to see if Vanessa made my dick hard.

She didn't.

The only thing she did was get in my damn way when Rhys thought he was about to take my girl home and get lucky.

Not a freaking chance.

Not while I'm still here.

So fuck Rhys.

Fuck the entire baseball team who thinks they are going to take a run at my girl when I leave.

It's not happening.

Getting up and choosing to ignore Thad's texts, I throw on some sweats and a semi-clean shirt, while I wait for Anniston in the kitchen. She has to forgive me after the birthday present I obsessed over for months.

She has to forgive me, right?

Sighing, I pour Anniston a cup of coffee just the way she likes it. Anxiety courses through me as the minutes tick by and her bedroom door never opens. The irrational part of me wants to barge through her door and tell her she's being ridiculous. We fight all the time. Last night got a little heated, but I didn't mean it. I was wrong; I know that. I embarrassed her—made her feel unwanted and unloved. She should know she isn't though. I can't take back my actions or the words I let free.

I'm sorry for what I did.

When I hear the remarks the guys say about her… I can't handle it. Rage overcomes me, and all I want to do is snatch her up and run. Flee to the mountains or take an impromptu road trip so the guys will forget her. Hell, I'd even support her if she wanted to wear baggy clothes. But that's wishful thinking. Anniston is unforgettable. I know that, and now guys are making their move since I'm so close to graduating.

I scrub a hand down my face and scowl at her still closed door.

Don't do this, Ans. Don't leave me.

Unable to deal, I throw her now cold cup of coffee into the sink and hear the cup shatter. I pause, listening for the click of the door to see if she comes out to yell at me.

She doesn't.

"Mr. Von Bremen, can I see you for a moment?"

Motherfucker.

I nod to Professor Cline and sling my laptop in my bag with more force than necessary. After Anniston blew off our run together for the first time in years, my day went to shit. Everything went wrong. First, I ran out of shampoo and had to use hers. Now, all I can smell is her, and it's driving me fucking crazy. As if that wasn't enough punishment, I forgot my shake—because Anniston didn't fucking make it!—and I was starving. So I figured, fuck it, today was shot anyway, and bought a jelly-filled doughnut, which I promptly spilled all over my shirt. I had to change into my dirty workout shirt from yesterday because, again, Anniston didn't change out my bag!

And now, to top off the shit-tastic day, Professor Cline needs to see me after class. I already know what he wants to talk about, and I'm not in the mood. This is all Anniston's fault. Sure, I said some mean shit and made her feel like an STD in a church choir, but seriously, she knows I didn't mean it. My temper gets out of hand sometimes. This isn't the first time this has happened.

Professor Cline clears his throat, and I realize everyone has cleared out, leaving the two of us. Grudgingly, I lumber down the steps to the front of the room where his desk sits off to the side. I slide my bag down to the floor, certain this won't be a short conversation.

"You wanted to see me, sir?"

I'm uncomfortable, okay? Anytime a teacher wants to discuss my condition, I break out into hives. Maybe he doesn't want to talk about my ADHD? Maybe he wants to tell me he appreciates my lack of discipline this morning and wants me to help teach next week's class. It could happen.

"Yes," he starts, lowering his glasses and matching my gaze.

He doesn't want me to teach a class.

"I wanted to talk about your quiz this morning."

I nod, remaining nonchalant as if I have no idea why he wants to talk about my quiz. I showed up to class and partook in the quiz and even turned it in. If you really think about it, I've handled my shit today. I really don't see an issue.

When Professor Cline realizes I won't be much of a contributor to this conversation—I'm no fool—he sighs and tries again. "Theo, you seemed very…" ADHD? Hyper? Pissed? Fucking lost? "—distracted this morning."

Distracted is a nice way of putting it. I'm a fucking wreck. Fighting with Anniston has a way of fraying my soul—unravelling it slowly so it reminds me when I leave for Washington, I won't keep but a thread with me. All of it will remain here, wrapped around Anniston's finger. I will be lost and without the only person who has ever given a shit about me.

"Yes, sir," I mumble, masking the aggravation with a cough. "I had a rough morning and forgot my medicine." Because Anniston wouldn't open her damn door!

The professor flashes me a look like he understands it's Anniston's fault too.

"How about you come back tomorrow and retake it? I'll average the two scores." He frowns, scratching his beard. "I'd hate to see all of your grades decline at the end of your senior year."

I don't really give a shit, but grades mean a lot to Anniston and my father, so I work hard to make them proud.

"That'd be great, sir. Thank you."

Professor Cline smiles, the lines of his forehead prominent, and stands, extending his hand to me. "You've been a refreshing change in my class this year, Mr. Von Bremen. I wish you luck in the minor leagues."

I nod, swallowing down the ball of dread that settles in my stomach. The date on my plane ticket is a constant reminder of what I'm leaving behind.

"Thank you, sir."

Yeah, that's all I can say.

I want out of this room.

I want away from this school.

I want to go home and grab my girl and shake her.

She deserves it.

I don't shake her.

She's not even home when I get there. It pisses me off further. So rather than taking the high road and study or run off the aggression, I drink.

I'm a simple man.

One beer turns into four, and since I didn't eat—again, Anniston's fault—I have a good buzz going on by the time she finally graces me with her presence. The door clicks shut softly, and I keep staring at the TV like I don't hear her come in.

"What are you doing home? Didn't you have practice?"

Yep. Blew that off.

Again, her fault.

I don't answer her and, instead, take a swig of beer.

Out of the corner of my eye, I see her set her bag down on the table and pick up the quiz I bombed.

"You failed your economics quiz?"

And the award for the most observant person in this room goes to…

"Theo."

Her tone goes from soft and concerned to hard and angry. Good. I want her angry. I want her to feel just like me.

"Are you planning to ignore me all day?"

Yes. Yes, I am. How do you like dem apples, Anniston? Sucks, doesn't it?

I turn the volume up on the TV, purposely drowning out the sigh she drags out for my benefit. The next chug of beer goes down bitterly. I hate being an asshole to her, but dammit, she started this. She fucked up my whole day by being mad at me. Anniston knows I act like a dick when she's around other guys. Shit. Why does she think she doesn't get asked out very often? Everyone in this town knows she's mine.

Yes, I don't deserve her.

But I'm selfish and I don't give two shits what anyone else thinks. I want her, and when I pull my shit together, I'll have her. Just not right now.

The door slams, and I realize my tactic of drowning out any more of her attempts to talk to me worked all too well.

Way to go, Theo. Piss on the last few days you have with her.

Argh!

My fingers squeeze around the neck of my beer. I want to throw the fucker into the kitchen. I feel sure I could get it into the sink. The shatter will make me feel better.

But I don't.

Don't ask me why.

Maybe I'm tired of acting like a dick, throwing tantrums when Anniston doesn't see things my way. Or maybe I don't want to clean up the mess I would make by throwing the bottle. Not only with the glass, but between Anniston and I. Something has embedded itself into our relationship, and frankly I'm curious and scared to see where it takes us.

My body, tight with anxiety, flexes when I fold over my knees and stand. Yes, I'm throwing the bottle away like a good boy. Someone should tell Anniston. I could use some praise right now. My mood sucks.

Passing by the table, I see my test glaring back at me, but one thing is different. My name, scrawled in blue ink, is smeared like someone spilled something on it or someone was… crying.

Fuck me.

Chapter Thirteen

Anniston

He made me a memory book out of all the old photos. Dozens of photos scattered the pages in the most unorganized way. There weren't any cute captions or sweet sentiments. Just photos. As many as he could fit on the pages.

It was a complete mess.

But it gutted my soul.

Because in the back, scrawled in his terrible writing, was a note.

Ans,

I know you don't always like to celebrate your birthday. So I made you a book that celebrates something different instead.

This book marks every year that you've put up with my shit.

Every year when I was an asshole—which was a lot.

Every year when you made me laugh, and every year I held back tears because you needed me to be strong.

Yes, this book is about me.

I'm joking.

This book is to remind you of how truly wonderful you are. How truly amazing you really are.

You don't give yourself enough credit, babe.

But I see the change.

Every day, I see you blossom into the woman your mother and grandparents would be proud of.

You are my biggest inspiration.

You are Katniss fucking Everdeen.

May you always remember what you mean to me.

Happy birthday, my love.

Theo

I cried for hours looking at those pictures. There wasn't enough concealer in the drug store to cover up those bags. He made me a memory book. On those pages were pictures from when we were fourteen until just recently. He wants me to remember him when he leaves.

Somewhere between running alone and finding his exam on the counter made me realize something.

We failed.

Not in the sense of an exam but in our friendship. I failed him. He's always been there for me, and no matter what happened last night, I let him down. Sure, he acted like a royal asshole, but I knew when I saw the coffee splattered in the sink this morning, he was sorry.

I don't understand why we do this to each other. Why do we bury these feelings until they overflow and we can't stop the explosion that spills out? I knew leaving with Rhys would piss Theo off, and if I'm being completely honest, I wanted to make him mad. He pissed me off too.

But being petty should not have been the answer. I opened a portal I knew he would jump through. He thinks I don't see him giving his teammates a death glare every time they look in my direction, but I do. I see him. And after our night together, I thought things would change between us. But they didn't. Everything went back to the way they were.

I was angry.

I was hurt.

I was heartbroken.

I was a fool.

All Theo and I have ever been is friends. I let my head poke through the clouds and try to ruin the friendship we had built over time. He's not my boyfriend. I have no right to make him jealous. Okay, so I do a little. I'm the one who has dealt with his shit every day for the past eight years. Yes, me. Not Kim from the softball team or Rachael from Sigma Kappa Blah-Blah. It's been me. All me. Von Bremen, whether he wants to admit or not, is mine. He was eight years ago, and he is now. Kim and Rachael are only distractions from the truth. He's mine. He knows it. I know it. And I'm tired of this back and forth.

Thinking of the man purposely ignoring me on the sofa, I toss off my shirt, change into my sports bra and one of his old jerseys, and slide on some leggings. I know what we need, and right now, we need what brought us together in the first place.

Baseball.

In the hallway, I grab his bat bag and pull on his hat. I look the part, and when I drop the bag at my feet in the living room, his head snaps up, his eyes roaming all over my body. I see the need in his eyes.

"Get your shit, Von Bremen."

He doesn't say anything to my demand, but he quirks a brow and tamps down the almost smile he nearly lets loose.

What did I tell you? We need this.

"What if I'm not in the mood?" he taunts.

"What if I hit you with this bat for getting on my nerves more than necessary today?"

A slow smile tugs at the corner of his full, pouty lips, and it shoots straight to my heart, making me feel shittier for not talking to him this morning. We could have saved ourselves a shit-ton of stress today. But then I would have missed this smile, so I'm thinking it was worth it in some ways.

"You have two minutes to change before I leave without you."

He acts casual as he pulls himself off the sofa like he doesn't give a shit if I leave him or not. His cut forearms flex when he slides them into the front pocket of his jeans before stepping toe to toe with me.

"Do I have any clothes left to change into?" he murmurs with a victorious gleam in his eye.

I scoff. "Don't flatter yourself. All of my clothes are dirty." I roll my eyes to hide my true feelings—I love wearing his clothes. I love his last name hanging on my back. Silly, I know, but it's how I feel.

He hums and grins, brushing past me. "I smell bullshit."

"You're about to smell bullshit when I put my foot up your ass. Hurry up, Von Bremen, before I lose my patience."

For God's sake, get away from me before I hug you and tell you I'm sorry for not running with you this morning.

Finally, he retreats to his room to change, and I'm able to settle down my hormones. Seriously, why am I so emotional today? Theo and I fight all the time. We're two alphas; we always butt heads.

You know why, screams the stupid part of my brain.

It's because he's about to leave me… and maybe because I love him more than a friend.

Before I can fully analyze my emotions, Theo barrels down the hall, scooping up his bat bag from the floor, and heads to the door, throwing over his shoulder, "Come on, McCallister, let's get to this."

And just like that, we are back to our old selves.

"Out!"

I give the two freshmen an apologetic smile as they gather their gear quickly and exit the batting cages like their asses are on fire.

"You didn't have to make them leave," I argue with the idiot who is filling two pitching machines with quarters. He stops cold and whips around to face me.

"Yes, I did." He flashes me an ugly look that makes me want to throw a ball at his pretty face. "I don't need any witnesses for what I'm about to say to you, McCallister."

So it's like that, is it?

He has something to say, huh? Well, so do I.

I snatch a bat from his bag and forego a helmet. Shit is about to get real out here.

"All right, Von Bremen, let's settle this." I shove him out of my cage and hook the latch. For a moment, we just stare at one another, separated by only chain-linked fencing. His blue eyes are fierce, like he can't decide if he wants to shake me or hug me. He settles for a growl and a bat, taking his spot a few seconds later in the batter's box.

"Get ready." He nods at the machine in warning.

I roll my eyes, squaring my shoulders and adjusting my stance. Before the first ball is launched out of the machine, I briefly wonder what speed setting he put my pitches on.

When the first ball zings past my face, I jump back. Obviously, he set my pitches just as fast as his. But whereas I missed the first pitch, Theo doesn't. The crack of his bat echoes in the open air.

"You're an asshole," I say aloud, readying for the next pitch and missing it.

"This should not be a surprise to you."

The sound of wood making contact with the ball and his smart-ass tone causes me to grind my teeth together.

"Yes, Theo, I know you have asshole tendencies. However, you were especially cruel last night. You had no right to talk to me that way. I'm not your personal property."

Another ball smashes into the fence, but he doesn't answer, which only makes me want to argue with him more.

Forget hitting the ball, I turn to his side of the fence and smash my bat against it. He doesn't even flinch.

"Theo!"

A fastball whizzes past him, and he misses for the first time. In hindsight, I should have seen his reaction coming, but when he slams his bat against the fence, his chest heaving with every drag of air, I realize I flipped his figurative switch.

His fingers curl around the chain, and he all but growls, "Rhys was going to fuck you on the community mattress in that shithole of a house he lives in. Is that what you wanted, Anniston? To wallow around in all the fluids of the women before you? Is that what you fucking wanted?"

His voice raises, and he slams the bat against the fence again, causing me to flinch.

"I can handle myself," I say calmly. Theo needs to chill the fuck out; his face is red, and he looks like he could destroy property with the bat in his hand.

An evil laugh filters through the humid air, clinging to the back of my neck.

"Is that right?" he sneers, unlatching the gate and barging his way in. His cheek twitches with barely controlled rage, and I take an instinctive step back. "Tell me, Anniston," he mocks, crowding me against the fence, the fastballs whizzing past his head like small rockets. "Tell me what you would have done if Rhys had you in this position."

Before I can even digest his words, Theo shoves me against the fence, his hips pinning me to the harsh metal. He drops the bat, grabbing my hip with one hand and my jaw with the other.

"Fight me, Anniston. Show me how you would have fought him off."

A stupid noise escapes me. Damn him.

Damn.

Him.

I try shoving him away, but he's too strong and I get zero traction.

"Fine!" I scream at the stupid smirk on his face, but he doesn't let me go. "I knew you would come after me," I admit, hitting him in the shoulder. I hate that he makes me crazy. I hate I care if he goes out with other girls. I hate I love him and I'm not sure he feels the same.

Tears well in the corner of my eyes, but I don't let them fall. Not even when he frowns.

"You wanted me to come after you?"

I nod.

It's the truth. I wanted to hurt him like he hurt me, but now I just admitted I was a jealous roomie, my heart sinks to my toes. What am I doing? Am I really about to tell Theo I was jealous that he was with Vanessa?

"I, uh… I was—" Madly in love with you. "—hormonal. And tired." I pat him on the chest and force him to the side, so he doesn't step back into the pitches. "I'm sorry. I knew Rhys was a dickbag. I think I was just hurt. It wasn't how I wanted to spend my birthday. I'm sorry for worrying you."

Smooth, Anniston, real smooth.

Theo looks stunned, scratching his chin and running a frustrated hand through his hair.

"How did you want to spend your birthday?"

I shrug. "I wanted to go watch the Braves one last time with you." I shrug again. "I guess it doesn't matter now." Squatting, I pick up his bat and tip my chin at the ball machine. "You want to hit some more?"

He shakes his head, a frown firmly planted on his face.

"I'm sorry. I should have run with you this morning," I add. The bat hangs heavy in my hands, and the guilt over his test hits me. "I should have studied with you and reminded you to take your medicine this morning."

The bat eases from my hand before it's replaced by his warmth.

"Look at me," he demands.

It's hard because the tears really want to fall, but I hold firm and keep them sealed up where they belong and lift my head to meet the concerned depths of his royal blues.

"I'm sorry for being an asshole and making you feel like a little girl unable to fend for yourself. I was so worried about you, and the thought of Rhys—"

His mouth is like a semitruck barreling down the freeway when it crashes into mine. This kiss isn't soft. It's angry and brutal. Our teeth clash and our tongues fight for the upper hand. And then it's over as quickly as it began.

Damn you, Von Bremen.

He steps back, his lips wet with the evidence that we, in fact, just kissed. And by the way his jaw is working, he wants to do it again.

And again.

Until we're writhing and naked beneath each other.

Okay, I don't know that. I'm just assuming he feels the same as me right now—a whole lot of horny.

Patience, Anniston.

"Did you really think I would let Rhys fuck me?" I ask, hoping to change the subject and calm us down.

Really. Rhys has fucked everything with a heartbeat, and even that may be a stretch. Some of the girls tearing out of the frat house look like they might burst into flames under the sunlight.

Theo sighs, fidgeting with the woven bracelet on his wrist.

"I promised Hines I would always look out for you."

Do not make a noise, even if you want to slap him and run to the car and leave his considerate ass. Is that really why he came after me? Because he promised my grandfather to always look out for me? He didn't come because he hated to see me with another man?

Sighing, I plaster a fake smile on my face and tap his shoulder.

"He would be very proud of you."

It's true. Theo was the grandson Hines always wanted. It's just…. It doesn't matter. Theo will never admit he loves me, and maybe I'm wrong. Maybe I misread this whole situation. Maybe he really is a great friend, and in a couple of days, I'll lose him either way.

So really, if I think about it, telling Theo how I really feel wouldn't be so terrible, would it?

Of course it would. How many movies have we seen where best friends ruin their relationship by bumping uglies? Yet…

"Hines would have beaten your ass, and mine, if he knew what we've done these past four years of school," he muses, a small chuckle rumbling in his chest.

I shrug. Technically, I haven't done near the amount of sinning Theo has.

"I feel like he would beat your ass the most," I say, smiling before adding, "I merely flirted with sin. You unzipped your pants, jerked off on it, and then flipped it off while you fingered its sister."

His face scrunches up like he tasted something nasty. "That is the dumbest metaphor I have ever heard."

"Don't care. It's the truth."

One hundred percent the truth. Theo has always been the bad boy with the gooey center.

"Whatever," he says unaffected. "I'm sorry anyway. I shouldn't have said those things to you. I was an asshole. Forgive me?"

Of course I forgive him. It isn't the first time he's said something mean, but he's holding back what he truly wants to say.

I think.

"Of course." I extend my hand, and he swats it away with a glare.

"You're lying," he accuses flatly. An exasperated noise escapes me, but he cuts it off. "I know you, Anniston McCallister. Better than you know yourself."

He's really reaching now.

If he really knew me, then he would know I do forgive him. That's not the issue here. The issue is, he's a little liar. Theo Von Bremen did not yank me from Rhys for my grandfather.

He did it for selfish reasons.

Reasons, I plan on using to get what I want.

"I'm not lying. I said I forgive you, and to prove it, you can buy dinner tonight."

He eyes me suspiciously but starts bagging up our gear.

I watch him watching me. He knows I'm up to something.

And he would be correct.

It's time I find out just how shallow you have to play in the friend zone to make it around all the bases to score.

Two salads and two showers later, Theo and I are back in our routine of lounging on the sofa watching game footage. I spent the whole car ride debating on the right time to ask him my favor.

I decide that there was no time like the present.

I need him to know I don't want to be friends anymore. It's as simple as that.

"Theo," I say, pausing the game.

He turns, catching my gaze.

"Hmm?"

You can do this, Anniston. Just tell him.

"I'm a virgin."

There. See? Nothing to it.

Except, Theo makes a strangled sound.

"Okay," he drawls, his face looking pink tinged. "Why are you telling me this?"

That is the question, isn't it?

"Because I want you to take my virginity."

Does Theo take Anniston up on her offer?

Read *Commander!*

Like all of my books, it's free in Kindle Unlimited.

Love *Pitcher*? Want to read more from this series? All books are standalones and are free in Kindle Unlimited.

Other books by
KRISTY MARIE

21 Rumors
A Romantic Comedy Series- All novels are standalone and feature different couples with crossover characters

IOU
The Pretender
The Closer
21 Rumors Box Set

The Commander Legacies
A Second-Generation Contemporary Series- All novels are standalone and feature different couples with crossover characters

Rebellious

Commander in Briefs
A Contemporary Series- All novels are standalone and feature different couples with crossover characters

Pitcher

Gorgeous
Drifter
Interpreter
Commander in Briefs Box Set

In the Hands of the Potters

A Contemporary Series- All novels are standalone and feature different
couples with crossover characters

The Potter
The Refiner
#3 Coming Soon
#4 Coming Soon

For more information visit www.authorkristymarie.com

Come hang out in my Facebook reader group,
Kristy's Commanders, for exclusive content and sneak peaks of
my newest releases.

Sign up to receive updates on all my new releases and
participate in juicy giveaways.

Check out my website and purchase signed copies of your
favorite paperback.

Follow me!

Amazon: www.amazon.com/author/mariekristy

BookBub: www.bookbub.com/authors/kristy-marie

Instagram: www.instagram.com/authorkristymarie

Facebook: www.facebook.com/authorkristymarie

Twitter: www.twitter.com/authorkristym

Goodreads: www.goodreads.com/author/show/17166029.Kristy_Marie

Acknowledgements

Thank you for picking up this book and taking a chance on my words. I realize your time is precious. It's my mission to always give you a memorable story worth those precious hours of alone time. So, thank you for spending your evenings, mornings, or lunch hour with my characters. You, the reader, are what keeps stories alive.

It's never without sacrifice to write a book. Namely, your own sanity. But when you're surrounded by the best readers and friends a girl could ask for, that loss of sanity turns into a full blown orgy of craziness in the best way. In no particular order, these are the crazies that held me together for this wild ride.

My street team. You ladies are the definition of dedication. Your post and excitement bring tears to my eyes. You keep me going.

Jessica, I kinda run out of things to say to you. So I'll make this one short and let Theo tell you how we feel—because I'm weird and you'll laugh. "No takebacks. You'll always be our girl."

Jaime, did we just become best friends? Gah! I sure hope so. Otherwise all my texts seem a bit stalkery. Thank you for not blocking me and reading this book about nine billion times in between talking baseball shit with me. You know it turns me on.

Ajee, I tried really hard not to whine this time. I think I made it to strike two. Thanks for not calling me out. I heart you hard.

Sarah P., I think we should make a list of how many times I asked you to read things on short notice. It has to be brag-worthy by now. Thank you for being my go-to. You rock!

Laura, thank you for making me feel like my words are picture worthy. You're always there to support me and boost my confidence like a mofo with your epic teasers. I have so many plans for you. Are you ready?

Sarah S., I'm so impressed you still want to beta read for me. I felt sure I scared you off earlier. But nope, you are superhuman. Thank you for guiding my stories and keeping me grounded with constructive support only to obliterate it by posting beautiful teasers that make me feel like I wrote something epic. I heart you.

To my betas who are always my biggest supporter and group therapy when I need it, I love you guys. Each and every one of you.

Autumn. Thanks for always hanging in there when I forget to tell you things or let my inner control demon loose. You are a hero for all the bullshit you deal with. Don't think it goes unnoticed.

Virginia and Rebecca of Hot Tree Editing. You're stuck with me forever. The end. There is no negotiating this. I CANNOT live without you.

Letitia, why are you so phenomenal? Every cover is magnificent. Especially this one. Thank you for enduring my million messages. I love you!

Stacy, of Champagne Formats, you will be forever mine. Seriously, everything you do is gold. Thank you so much for being patient with me and always making time for last-minute crap.

To Bex, thank you for making magic and cracking the code on this whole website business and creating all the beautiful graphics for Pitcher. You're a Rockstar!

A special thank you to the best reader group ever established: Kristy's Commanders. You guys are a second family that I actually want to talk to.

And a very special thank you to Andi and Sofia, who every week, wow me with their love and dedication to this series with their beautiful edits. Words will never be enough to describe what you do to my heart. Never.

About the Author

Kristy Marie lives in Georgia with her husband and three children. When she isn't reading or writing, you can find her at SunTrust Field cheering on the Atlanta Braves.

Made in the USA
Monee, IL
14 June 2023